ABOUT THE AUTHOR

Dr. David S. Cantor is an Argentinean-born physician graduated from Buenos Aires University and trained as a gastroenterologist in the United States.

He is a Clinical Professor of Medicine, Past President of the Medical Staff and Medical Director of the Department of Gastroenterology of the Huntington Hospital in Pasadena, California, Past president of the Southern Society for Gastrointestinal Endoscopy and Past President of the Pasadena Medical Society, among many other positions.

He wrote one textbook of Gastroenterology and Hepatology, co-authored another and recently published *The Book of Good Health*, directed to the general population.

He has published 50 scientific papers and has been a co-founder and Editor of Acta Gastroenterologica Latino Americana.

He co-founded *Health Alert*, a medical newsletter.

He retired from private practice and is now, at 77 years of age, writing short stories and essays. He received the James N. Gamble award, among other distinctions.

DAVID S. CANTOR

DEATH AND OTHER NUISANCES

*A
Tribute to
Life*

Pippa Publications

Copyright 2013 by David S. Cantor.

All rights reserved.

For information about permission to reproduce sections from the book, write to alidacho@aol.com

Printed in the United States of America

Cover by Laura Kaplan Lirman

To my great-grandparents, my grandparents, my parents, my wife and children, their spouses and my grandchildren, their children and the children of their children

Contents

Prologue...10

Death...14

Ghost: An Education...18

Twenty-Two Seconds...21

Celebrating the Fart...29

A la Recherche du Bialy Perdu...37

Ecstasy...52

A Love Letter...55

Hindu Philosophy: The Sharing Stone...73

The Gold Medal...78

A New Word for a New World...82

A Story of Love and Other Coincidences...91

Aging Gracefully: A contradiction...109

An Ordinary Man...116

Spinocrates Junior the III (1940-1999)...126

Spinocrates Senior the II (1922-1970)...127

Back to School...128

Obituaries...137

Birth Announcement...139

Notice from the Editor...141

Deconstructing the Establishment...143

Two Sisters and One Brother...147

Exquisite Synchronicity...154

Inspiration...158

Facts and Statistics...166

Finally...172

Friends...183

Garbanzo Beans...185

Global Economy...189

I Am Okay...192

In Defense of Literary Fraud and Plagiarism...195

Messi...199

The Art of Thievery...202

Historical Quiz...226

The Carriage...229

The Cupcake Syndrome...235

A Detective Story...240

The Imaginary Patient...245

The Kingdom of Others...258

The Uncontrollable Persistence of a Routine...269

Three Centuries...272

Welcome Back Salomon...277

Why I Worship my Psychoanalyst...279

PROLOGUE

Soon, I will be arriving at the ultimate life experience called death, which made me aware that now is the time to be authentic and free. One way to make my finitude less predetermined is to get a sense of what the end of all ends means. I cannot do it by relying on my philosophical or religious understandings since everything has been already told, so I decided to concoct stories to ponder the road that takes us to the end of human life, which comes in many shapes and forms.

Our own death is a funny thing if we don't fear it or deny it. When I was fifty-six years old I died and was brought back to life after two minutes. Death was interrupted by a paramedic who used two electric paddles to reverse the situation. So I have a certain authority to write about this issue. Much to the disappointment of many, I did not have a near-death experience and found the tales of such occurrences rather unlikely, improbable, naïve or stupid.

I don't know how I am going to react when I confront the arrival of such an illustrious host. Writing this book is part of my preparation.

You may, in these stories, find the meaning of death; your perception may be different from mine or anybody else's.

What bothers people is not knowing the way they may depart from this world. As a physician, I have witnessed how brutal and unforgiving the process of reaching the end can be. Paradoxically, many times, it is made that way by the ones that are supposed to preserve our wellbeing, like some oncologists - who with the excuse of prolonging life for few weeks or months - may subject patients to all kinds of suffering by administering medications to slow the process of dying, at the same time that they make patients lose weight, feel weak, lose hair, experience nausea and diarrhea, and aggravate their suffering. Other times, family members demand to keep a dear one alive, hoping that they may beat the grim statistics. It never happens.

I have seen this hundreds of times, fought with some of the perpetrators and unfortunately proved that I was always right.

Lately I have found myself reading the obituaries in the newspaper; I do this with amusement and curiosity. On January 30, 2013, I read in the Los Angeles Times about 5 illustrious people that passed away: Don Cornelius, the creator of "Soul Train", at age 75; John Rich, a TV and Film director, 86; Harry Carey Jr., the actor, 91; Jean Harris, of infamous fate, 86; Norman Schwarzkopf, the commander of "Desert Storm", at age 78 - an average age of 83.2 and a nice age of finality if you are 45 years old, but a horrible one if you are 80 and healthy. There is some hope: Rita Levi-

Montalcini, the Nobel Prize laureate, who discovered the nerve growth factor and was also a Senator for Life in Italy, died at the age of 102. These are games that I love to play.

But by golly! They are keeping Ariel Sharon, the ex-Prime Minister of Israel alive. He has been in a vegetative state since suffering a stroke in January of 2006; this shows that modern technology is well advanced, as is the idiocy of human beings.

Writing is an outlet to express my sorrow and joy for me and others.

The 'nuisances' part of the title of the book refers to other stories and poems. I will let them speak for themselves; they represent different shades of life.

Some have asked me: Why you are writing about death?

I am 77 years old; this gives me a license to write about it. Paradoxically I do it to celebrate life, which I worship.

When you are walking in the jungle and know that at the end there is a lion waiting, you can spend all your energy fearing what the lion may do to you when you reach your last stop or keep walking and admiring the green of the trees, the elegance of the forest, the sunbathing of the white-headed langurs, the chirping of the birds and the splendor of the habitat. Don't fear the lion; sooner or later he will become an abstraction. Reality is the jungle.

The lion has strength, beauty and vigor, he is expedient and majestic, but he is not riding my existence. I am the master of my providence.

The book is a tribute to my ancestors, the ones that shaped my personality, provided joy, instigated my vivacity and gave me the energy to become what I became: a serious man who easily becomes one that loves a funny story, a joke, a tease.

Because my calling in life is to help others, I trust that you will get enjoyment from the book, as well as an attitude of refined contemplation of what is ahead for all of us.

Death

When I am here

She is not;

When she is here

I am not.

The encounter, then,

Is not be feared.

There is no encounter

At all.

Shed no tears;

I am lost to the wind.

When the waves retreat

That piece of sand is me.

You see the moon:

Perhaps I am there,

Climbing

Or walking

Or dreaming

Or flying -

Perhaps that is me.

They will ask,

"Is he gone?

I thought he was

Asleep

In the morning quiet

Or the tranquility of the night."

That stillness,

That peace,

That silence -

Is it for real?

Does it mean?

That he is happy

Where he is?

Do not shed any tears;

I will not be back.

You care

For a while;

Cry if you want.

I will not be back.

Sing if you wish,

Like the birds sing.

It is the same;

I am gone.

I will miss you

More than you think.

For you,

Life

Will go on.

Now that I am gone,

Existence is

A soul,

A feeling -

This is my essence.

And you,

A soul,

A feeling,

A noise,

A smell.

You and I -

We are the same.

No need for tears.

I am gone;

I am here.

Ghost: An education

My name is Vivian Cunningham, the first and only daughter of Earl James Cunningham and Countess Beatrice Ness. I was born in Argyll on July 7, 1432 in my parent's castle, located in the north side of town. The castle was fortified by thick stone walls with an outlandish architecture that was the envy of our frequent visitors, the honorable members of the Scottish kingdom. Paradoxically, it was this fortification that gave us fame and social recognition that I used to find my demise. The memories of my childhood in the prairies and slopes of the castle garden are still with me, but that is another story.

One day, precisely on July 7, 1452, as I was leaving our private chapel, on a day of prayers and celebration, I developed a strange and deep exhilaration that made me run to one of the towers, from which I jumped to my death. A soldier of the fortress witnessed my leap and yet when he looked down there was no corpse and the ground was generally undisturbed. He wisely chose not to reveal what he saw, fearing that he would not be believed. My disappearance gave pain and consternation to my parents and my friends, because I was a loving, kind and gracious being. Soon I learned that I died a different kind of death, one that few individuals experienced: I became a ghost, one that will inhabit this world forever. I am now 581 years old, doing what I have to do with the same sense of delight and passion as when I jumped into the abyss.

This writing, the first by a ghost, is the bequest that I offer to mankind as homage to their persistent quest for knowledge. I am doing this somewhat reluctantly because I am afraid that I may curtail the elation that discovery brings. Yet I am convinced that there is no way that anybody may even remotely achieve comprehension of who we are.

We live in a space where there is no shape or form, where there are no dimensions, no physical material, no water and no air. We are ethereal in a way that cannot be defined. We cannot be seen, cannot be touched and yet we interact with you, trying to save you from other creatures that intermingle with the inhabitants of your world. We are the angels; they are the demons. We fight a constant battle for your sake; sometimes we win, and sometimes we lose. We lose when your free will tilts the balance of power to the wrong side. Although we feel no physical pain, we are nurtured by happiness and discouraged by sadness. No other feelings or emotions: happiness ensues in after a smile and sadness after a tear.

We don't haunt houses, don't maim and don't make things happen. We don't live in cemeteries or under your bed, nor are we responsible for fatal accidents. We are assigned only to you and although this may seem a contradiction, to everybody else.

Listen to what we have to say because we have been saying this from time immemorial; act upon what we preach when we are inside you and remember that ghosts are angels. Beware of the demons that inhabit the same space.

We are not in your prefrontal lobe or your heart, we are within you.

We exist because you exist. When you are gone, we will still be with your children and your children's children.

I did not jump to my end to end my life; I sprinted from my castle to be with mankind. I still keep my fortress; it is inside of me.

Don't try to prove that I exist; we are dogma and dogmas are indisputable.

Twenty-two Seconds

Before my demise, I was informed that upon my departure I would have 22 seconds to engage with whoever I would like; after that I would enter a celestial galaxy that would become my eternal destination.

I had been suffering from cancer and my body was wasting away; my pain was severe, mitigated only by potent analgesics. I could not eat, my breathing was laborious, and my connection with the external world was totally gone. I always wanted to die in a dignified way, but my attending physicians, although full of good intentions, took that option away from me. I was told that I had an intractable form of pancreatic cancer and I was treated with chemo and radiotherapy, not as a cure, but to prolong my life. What an irony! In their experience, this kind of treatment would allow me to live one to two additional years. They told me that the side effects of treatment were considerable, but could be controlled with medications. We discussed their recommendations with my family and decided to go for it; otherwise death would be visiting me soon. All my questions about the collateral effects of treatment were answered in the subjunctive which enabled the treating physicians to avoid any responsibility. As it turned out, I lost considerable weight, my muscle mass wasted away and in a few weeks my hair was gone with the wind.

The greatest harm was the loss of my decorum. I was no longer the guy with a strong personality, a classy style or an enviable presence. I am an expert in the field of biochemistry; many have enjoyed listening to my dissertations or have come to me for advice and orientation in their pursuits. This was not to be any longer.

Today, everything revolves around my disease. What I had cherished and nurtured all my life was gone before I was gone. The elation for music disappeared, the joy of reading was no longer there; I had an inversion of my senses: cold felt warm, and warm felt cold.

After being mutilated by the savagery of medical treatment, I understood that the end of life is better when it comes unannounced and is unexpected. Better for the receiver and for the others, because the drama of a slow, unrelenting end disappears.

None of my many doctors told me what was about to come to me. They hid the truth from me and my family as a way of shielding us from the dreadful reality. Were they dreading their own death?

The nausea and the vomiting were unrelenting for a few days after chemo; it somewhat improved through medications, but they have other obnoxious side effects. My appetite was gone and my favorite dishes couldn't bring it back. My cravings were replaced by aversion. My taste buds could no longer appreciate my wife's moussaka. My skin rash and blisters came little by little. I looked like a fish; Darwin was right.

First I needed a cane to walk, and then a walker; later, somebody to help me and finally only my bed could provide solace. Urinary incontinence and spilling of fecal material forced me to wear diapers, despite which I could not avoid the unsavory staining of the bed sheets.

How many people were involved in this conspiracy? My regular physician, my designated oncologist, two consultants, a radiologist, a skin doctor, a gastroenterologist, two urologists, four nurses, ten nurse's aides, four maids and occasional others. I had consented to be treated; in a way, I was part of the plot, I traded hope for a progressively humiliating end to my existence. I ended up being ashamed of myself because my cancer doctors had no shame. They did not say "that's enough" when it was enough.

It would be better to use different metrics to assess the progress of a patient. It should not be the anemia, the high white cell count, the abnormal liver tests, the metastasis that dictates treatment but rather the loss of self-esteem and self-respect should tell when is time to let it go.

In my final two days I was in a coma and my soul was preparing to enter a different dimension. In contrast with my body, which was a wreck, my inner self was intact. During the few hours before my exodus, I was visited by an ethereal, amorphous character to help me walk the walk to infinity. Before the end, I was going to be endowed with the happenings of the world since the moment I was born, September 2, 1940, until the last second of my life, June 3, 2013. I was to have an experience of total recollection.

My soul, *and only for 22 seconds*, I could choose for that short, ephemeral time to be with any person or in any place I wished.

I was going to be able to see, talk and feel while all other senses would disappear, since they would not be needed in my other new space.

I had so many choices:

My big hero was Mozart. His music has been a constant in my life. I was intrigued about the force of his creativity. Would it be him?

Baruch Espinoza's rational thinking was the theory that shaped my actions in life.

Charles Dickens the one that initiated in me the love for literature.

Michael Shermer, the American author, taught me the intricacies of pseudoscience and religion.

I admired Rene Favaloro, a pioneer in the cardiology field.

Kim Novak, the actress, aroused intense feelings when I was a young lad.

Albert Einstein, of course.

Nora Ephron, of course.

Chagall, of course.

My family, of course.

And so many others.

I came to realize the impact that hundreds of people had in forging who I am.

I elected to use the allotted 22 seconds to have an encounter with my father, who died at age 37, when I was five years old. My memories of him were real and imagined, sometimes implanted in me by his sisters, who loved him dearly. It was not an easy decision; I had many other people that I loved profoundly, yet this choice came upon me with total certainty.

My dad was a precocious first violinist in the Seattle Philharmonic. He married my mother when they were both twenty-four. She was a custom designer for the Royal Opera, a profession she gave up after I, her fourth child, was born.

My memories of him were fragmented. I remember going with him to rehearsals and being pampered by his musician colleagues. Dad would bring presents to all his children after coming back from his tours. His return was always a delight because we knew that he was going to be with us for many full days before going back to work.

I was often on his lap listening to thrilling tales of his adventures around the world. Going to the ice cream parlor was our summer treat. His kisses on my belly button would make me erupt in uncontrollable laughter. So many memories!

One day he had a heart attack and was gone forever. This I could not understand. I was perplexed but not sad because for a while I thought that dad was working in some distant place and would be back anytime, but anytime never came.

As I grew up, I understood that I was different from other boys: they had a father and I did not. My aunt Grace, who loved her brother dearly, would tell me stories about him and the family. He was the oldest sibling, was always teasing them, learned magic tricks when he was just a young man and made things disappear that would emerge later in unusual places. He was the one that initiated the pillow wars with his siblings every weekend.

He made his family- especially my grandfather - proud when at twenty-three years old he was given the position of first violinist in the Seattle Philharmonic. When he died, he left unfinished a violin that he was making; mother said that it was going to sound better than a Stradivarius.

Grace told me that Dad was certain that I would become a scientist because I had a keen sense of observation, and this I took as a mandate.

I had many dreams with my father. He was not dead; I saw him walking in San Francisco or driving a car or playing in an orchestra with hundreds of other violinists.

Fantasy and reality did not collide; he was always there.

As I was fading away, I chose those twenty-two seconds to bring him back.

He reappeared with his perpetual smile, the man I always remembered. This time, I was a young man just out of school. We looked at each other and without either of us saying a single word, we felt again the loftiness of our mutual adoration. He was proud of his Michael, and I was overjoyed that all this time I had been right. My father never died; he guided me through easy and difficult times in my life; he shared with me the jubilation I felt when my first child was born. He is the one that told me that ambition without ethics is a regretful purpose;

with him, I celebrated my achievements, and with him, I shed the tears that came with my failures.

When the twenty-two seconds were over, to my surprise, I realized that it was the longest span of time I ever experienced.

Little by little I became shapeless, and my soul blended into a new, promising space.

Celebrating the Fart

When I told my publisher that I wanted to write an essay about the fart, he became alarmed and asked me not to do it. He found the subject to be offensive and vulgar. I told him that I felt I have a sense of entitlement to write about this subject, since I am Board-certified in Gastroenterology and being now 77 years old, I have seen enough people doing it regardless of who they are, where they live or what their social status is. I suspect that even the Queen of England does it. He then asked me, *What would you like to achieve in writing about matters of the gut?* It was an unnecessary question, coming from a reputable publisher; one writes for reasons that the brain do not understand. He then told me to at least change the title to flatulence or digestive gas, at which time I proceeded to fire him – which, come to think about it, is another form of expulsion.

You know publishers: when you are an amateur they treat you with fake respect. Their letters of rejection are custom made; their excuses for not even accepting to read the rest of your manuscript are puerile. They always like what you have written *'but at this time we cannot take any more projects because we are overwhelmed by demand'*. No matter how polished and original your query letter may be, if you are not somebody you are nobody. If you are lucky, as I was, you may find one. He was a patient of mine, so he felt obliged to accept my first book about the adventures of a young, intrepid boy, Kestapii, who sailed solo around the world. He liked it, and when the book became a moderate success we became friends, until now.

Flatus, as we physicians politely call it, is a combination of swallowed air, ingested food that contains gases like nitrogen, carbon dioxide, methane and hydrogen, and the effect of bacteria on food residuals within the gut. The noise that arises when one expels flatus is a function of the speed of gas traveling through the intestine and the tightness of the anal sphincter. I am not going to expand any further the physiology and pathophysiology of flatulence, but rather explain aspects of farting in a personal, social and psychological context.

My first experience with interpersonal farting in the presence of a member of the opposite sex was during my honeymoon. I had a short period of courtship with my then-girlfriend, limited to holding hands, kissing and discussing the trivial things of daily existence.

When we were young and going to college, we were concerned about our careers and did not have much togetherness. When we graduated, we decided to get married right away to make up for lost time.

We had a simple wedding, not because we could not afford a more lavish and opulent one, but because a modest one conformed more to our personalities. That day Katherine was radiant and charming, with a demeanor of grace that she still holds. Kay (as I call her) has many other attributes beyond her appearance; she is smart, witty and charming.

We chose St. Bart's, a French island in the Caribbean, for our honeymoon. Kay worked at the Alliance Française, and one of the perks of her job was getting cheap tickets to any of the French territories.

St. Bart is unique, a small piece of land surrounded by an ever-changing color of the water of its 22 beaches, from dark blue to light-indigo to green turquoise; the sea is calm or rough depending on the location. We chose to go to windward beaches because they are suitable for surfing, our favorite sport.

The days passed fast. We spent nights indulging in the island's famous culinary treats. We loved their Creole cuisine; each evening we enjoyed more than we should have.

I remember that evening well. I had Oyster and Artichoke Bisque and Katherine Gumbo soup, which we followed with Crawfish with red beans and rice; as a final treat, beignets for me and peach cobbler for her.

That night I had to release gas badly, but out of respect and to keep the romanticism of our relationship intact, I abstained. My gut rebellion became extremely uncomfortable, even painful. I had to disappear into a private place to calm my upheaval. Apparently I was not the only one.

That ill-fated night, as we were in bed, my beloved Katherine passed a potent amount of gas that produced a crescendo of vibrating sound. To both of us, the resonance appeared endless; after the reverberation stopped, what followed was a scene from an Italian movie. Kay turned red like a red tulip; I turned white like a white tulip; after few seconds of silence we disintegrated into minutes and minutes of laughter. At that time, I knew that my love was unconditional. That set our personal connection on a plane of comprehension and humility. We were no longer the perfect picture we imagined, but two human beings with virtues and flaws.

From that day on we felt no need to disrupt the call of nature.

The episode brought a recollection of a long-gone experience I had with my sister's in-law.

When I was 14 years old, I was invited to have dinner at their place. I was their only guest. We were fond of each other. They both were teachers, music enthusiasts and very active in politics. They loved to talk and to show their erudition. That evening we discussed the advantages and disadvantages of my vocational aspirations. I got a lecture about the role of a physician in modern society, which indeed influenced my later decision.

Mauricio was an excellent cook; that day he prepared a succulent meal. The best part of dinner was the endless tales from their native Austria. We talked (they talked), we laughed and cried when he told how he left his parents behind after he moved to the States. After having dessert, this charming couple, who might have been in their mid-sixties, started silently pacing the room; all of a sudden, his wife passed wind, at which time I expected either some embarrassment or an apology. Instead Mauricio exclaimed, "Bravo Victoria, bravo!" Then it was his turn; with a face of satisfaction, he uproariously released an airy matter. "Bravo Mauricio, bravo!" Victoria asserted.

All done naturally, without inhibitions. Perhaps that was a European tradition. They had no social constraints, or if they did, they may have considered me part of their intimates, where these kinds of things are encouraged and permitted.

When this scene came back into my memory, I realized that over time Kay and I would transform the shyness and awkwardness of that moment into a ritual of care and protection.

The word fart has appeared in numerous novels, poems, historical accounts, radio and TV shows and has been used to describe, to offend or as a practical joke, since immemorial times, by well-respected people like Seneca, Homer, Benjamin Franklin, Jim Dawson, Hemingway, Rabelais and Aristophanes, to name just a few. In our contemporary era, doctors and mothers have decided that normal functions of the body should be talked about and even promoted, so farting became a subject of candid and open discussion, and a topic of children's books. In contrast, I and my siblings were punished if we dared to express so loudly the function of our intestines. Usually, the degree of punishment was proportional to the quality of the fart.

Going back to ancient history and to emphasize that there is nothing new under the sun, you may not know that the cushion-like device that we know as a whoopee cushion and use to play jokes on our friends was first introduced by the Roman Emperor Elagabulus during the Third Century. Elagabulus was openly irreverent to social conventions and sexual taboos.

The word fart in different languages has different meanings. For example, in English a person may be described, independent of his age, as an 'old fart', meaning boring or picky. In Spanish 'hablar al pedo' means talking nonsense or gibberish. In Italian there is a saying, 'Tromba di culo – Sano di corpo – Chi non scorreggia – E' un uomo morto', which loosely translated means 'Trumpet in your ass – Healthy body – He who doesn't fart – Is a dead man.'

In one of Geoffrey Chaucer's Canterbury Tales, one of the characters, Nicholas, in order to humiliate his rival Absolom, sticks his buttocks out of a window and humiliates him by farting in his face. Absalom then proceeds to take revenge by thrusting a hot blade between the cheeks of his behind.

It is refreshing that today we are dethroning farting from its previous irreverent meaning.

Blessed be Katherine, Mauricio and Victoria who pioneered the social acceptance of a much appreciated bodily function.

Long live: Fart, perdomai, pedere, pardate, perroaiti, perdet, peter, pedo, pezd and furzen.

Paraphrasing Cole Porter:

Birds do it,

Bees do it,

 Even educated fleas do it,

And lazy jellyfish do it,

Some Argentines without means do it,

The chimpanzees in the zoo do it,

Even you the reader may do it

And I might do it.

Let's do it!

A la Recherche du Bialy Perdu

I am a bread lover. I can trace the origin of my devotion to the fact that since my early childhood the tantalizing aroma of fresh baked bread invaded my senses and its exquisite flavor satisfied my cravings.

We lived in a barrio of small houses, of different shapes, colors and heights. There was no building code or if there was, it was never enforced. On the sidewalk there was one tall tree for each house that grew unattended and yet provided the cobblestone street a green arcade, a canopy for cars to drive through.

We lived about one block from the bakery. Each morning before going to school I went to fetch different breads that were prepared at 5 o'clock in the morning, baked in a brick oven and were ready to pick up at 7 when the bakery opened for business. The building, in contrast with the surrounding stores, was clean, with shiny tile floors; the display cabinets were full of pastries, cakes, sweet tarts, macaroons, napoleons and croissants. There were always lots of people waiting in line, a tribute of appreciation for fresh bread. The young clerks in their white uniforms serviced all of us with perpetual smiles.

On Sundays there was a festive ambience in the store; besides breads, we were also buying pastries, cakes and sweets - a sign that we were going to have a good time with family and friends. There were at least six varieties of bread that I remembered, probably many more: the *baguette* of sourdough confection; the *figazza* like a thick pita bread; the *loaf*, a chewy and soft bread; the *pebete,* a bun toasted on the outside and used for sandwiches; the *pan de miga*, a thin dough without crust invariably filled between layers with cheese, ham, tomatoes, lettuce, hard-boiled eggs, and red peppers; and *pan de campo*, a rustic version of bread. We ate mainly the baguette, which came in different sizes. When it was time to go to school or to work, our hunger was satisfied by whatever we ate for breakfast, which was always crowned by fresh bread.

My grandparents were bakers in Bialystok, Poland. They had a renowned store from 1875 till 1922, on Kupiecka Street, one that the few surviving Bialystokers that I have met still remember. My grandfather Moishe Mendl, a proud, stocky guy, was married to Linda (Sheine or Sonia) Kosovitski, a name that like many others has been distorted by

Customs clerks when people arrived from foreign lands and had to register their identity. Since most of them could not spell in Spanish, the employees went by phonetics. In Argentina we became Cantor, instead of Kantor, Goldstein became Gold, Peres became Perez - few were able to keep their names intact. Moishe and Sheine had 11 children: Isaac, Rachel, Bernardo, Felix (my dad), Fanny, Clara, Luba, Mina, Carlos, Leon and Jacobo (those were their Spanish names but they called each other by their Yiddish ones).

Moishe Mendl was heavyset, austere and a rigid disciplinarian, probably as his only way to maintain a certain order in his large family. His bakery was very successful and had a reputation that extended to neighboring counties; it was common to see, mainly on weekends, people from surrounding areas fetching bread and pastries.

All of his kids attended school, but during their spare time they worked in the bakery performing different tasks. Clara and Fanny were married and their husbands worked full time in the baking area.

My father Felix was born in 1904. He decided to immigrate to Argentina when he was 16. The Polish government had implemented a nasty pogrom against the Jews in 1906 that caused tremendous devastation; luckily my family was spared. My dad was to be called to serve as a conscript in the Polish army, but being aware of the mistreatment of young Jewish soldiers and the prevalent atmosphere of anti-Semitism, he decided, at such a young age, to go solo to Argentina. The United States would have been his first choice, but at that time immigration was closed to Polish people, so the bulk of people from Eastern Europe settled mainly in Argentina, Brazil, Bolivia and Chile. Felix promised to bring his entire family to his new land as soon as he could organize their departure and secure legal entrance.

When he announced his intentions to his father, he was surprised. *"You are too young son, you don't speak Spanish, and we have little money to give you,"* he said while being unable to hide his pride that Felix, his favorite son, decided to take on such an incredible enterprise, fearlessly and without hesitation. Moishe, who was always in command, for the first time relegated his role to his son. He never knew why from his eleven children he loved this young lad above all the others; indeed, love is a peculiar, unexplainable feeling. He consented and went with him to buy a one-way train ticket from Warsaw to Marseille and a one-way ticket from there to Buenos Aires on a cargo ship.

I wish I could have learned more stories about his younger years in his native land or the journey across the Atlantic or his early years in Argentina, but that was not to be the case.

In Argentina Felix first worked as a merchant, placing orders for leather gloves, scarves, hats, caps and related goods, which were manufactured in Buenos Aires and sold in 10 different provinces to which he traveled by train. At that time the trains were run efficiently by the British, who owned the whole rail system. I have seen many old photographs of his travels in the interior of the country, and from this I constructed a narrative that, true or not, became reality for me. He appeared to be a healthy, handsome man, not a young one. For whatever rationale, in my recollection, my parents and their contemporaries were always mature grown-ups. It may be that I had never seen them exercising or playing sports and saw them dressed very formally. Some of the pictures showed him and his friends dressed in hunting apparel and holding rifles. In others he was drinking yerba mate, a local drink, which is prepared from green dry leaves poured in a hollow gourd and shared with other people who drink it from a communal straw called bombilla. This showed how fast he had assimilated to his new country.

After five years of being on the road he saved enough money to buy a General Store in Resistencia, Chaco, a poor, neglected northern province which had seen many wars with its neighboring country Paraguay. Chaco had a great potential for farming and cattle raising but never reached full fruition. In the first decade of the 20th century, the province received immigrants from Canada, Russia and Germany.

The store was of middle size, located on the corner of two unpaved streets. It sold edibles for humans and all types of products for the fields, from animal foodstuff to goods for the harvest, wheel carts and hardware.

My dad married Sonia, an 18–year-old Bialystoker, who was introduced to him by his sister Fanny. They both worked as seamstresses in a dress shop. Sonia was a beautiful, shy, but determined young girl. Dad would not consent for her to work another single day in her life; instead, she devoted all her time to raising four children: a girl, a boy, a girl and another boy (me). Caring for us became her only mission in life, or so it appeared. If she had any other aspirations, I never knew. She was a practical, matter-of-fact person with an excellent sense of humor and prone to introducing frequent quotations in her conversations, which I never knew whether they were part of her native folklore or invented by her.

Felix's father had died in Poland from a heart attack, a condition that affected many of his descendants, a trait that we wear in spite of ourselves, one that today we try to reverse by 'doing the right things', like eating well (sometimes), exercising (sometimes) and avoiding stress (sometimes).

After few years Felix became a rich man. As promised, he brought his siblings to Argentina, with the exceptions of Isaac and Rachel, who decided to stay in Bialystok and later died in a concentration camp.

Our parents never talked about their life in Poland and we children knew very little about their past. It was peculiar; it made us a family without a history. War, the inhumanity of death camps and the extermination of Jews were topics that they did not dare or care to discuss. My family closed down on the Polish language and the memories of the past; they pushed away whatever could interfere with their renovation in their new chosen land. The remembrance of their heritage was manifested only through food and the Yiddish language. But even this was concealed; they only used it among themselves as the primary form of communication, any attempt that the children made to use Yiddish was forbidden. This was another way to become assimilated; they would not allow us to sustain a tribal identity.

In later years I resented this, because I could have used Yiddish to acquire a better Jewish identity.

After 12 years, dad sold the General Store, moved to Buenos Aires, Argentina's flourishing capital city, and built a textile factory in Nueva Pompeya, an industrial area 10 kilometers from our home. He chose those quarters, instead of Villa Lynch, the place where all the textile factories were run by his fellow Jews, and as such he became an innovator. In 1939 there was a big demand for textiles because of the Second World War, and in a few years he became a millionaire. The factory started with four looms, which slowly expanded to 24, and when he added a cotton processing plant, it became a large, respectable-sized manufacturing facility.

Felix was the family idol; his sisters and brothers adored him, probably because of his accomplishments and his generosity.

He was a self-taught man, the only one of the siblings who spoke Spanish without an accent, had excellent calligraphy and wrote with exceptional grammar. I remember Dad playing the violin (which I assumed he learned in Poland and perfected in Buenos Aires). Each evening before dinner, he would play his violin in the living room; we were forbidden to make noises that could interfere with the music. He was an avid reader and an antique collector.

My father was a very good man.

Dad got sick on a Sunday in Barrancas de San Isidro, in a club by the river, where we were spending the weekend. He died the following day; his heart gave up, a condition that has affected most of the men in my family. The emotional devastation caused by his demise was tremendous, but only for a while; as happened so many other times, the bereavement and grief was something that my mother was good at concealing, at least from us.

When father died I was five years old.

My mother married Felix's younger brother, as Jewish tradition dictates. Leon, a 24 year old chap with little education, became my stepdad and continued to be my uncle and the owner of a flourishing textile factory; he never could replace my father, not in the emotional sphere and not in the practical world.

We all went on without the presence of this powerful, intelligent, caring patriarch. After a while, we recovered the joy of life. In spite of their scarce education my aunts and uncles insisted that all the children in the family get a university degree. Some of us did, others became successful businessmen, and with few exceptions my female cousins, as was customary during those times, became housewives.

Our family gatherings during weekends were frequent, the grownups played dominoes or cards and the kids made lots of noise playing hide-and-seek, hopscotch, jumping rope, marbles, musical statues and - weather permitting - some street games. There was no television at that time, and digital was a word only reserved for fingers. At these reunions eating would always hold a central place. My aunts were the best cooks in the world. My uncle Saul, married to Clara, was a 'star' because, having been the master baker in Moishe Mendl's bakery, he brought his expertise from Bialystok.

Saul built a wood oven in his modest home in the outskirts of Buenos Aires. He did not care about esthetics and placed it at the center of the backyard, which from a distance looked like a sculpture. Saul would bake Challah for Sabbath and holidays, and always bread rolls and *bialystocher kuchens*. The *kuchen*, which we called *kuchelaj*, is known in the US as *bialy,* a chewy yeast bread roll with a depression in the center (not a hole like the bagel) filled with onions and/or poppy seeds or garlic. The aroma from baking this bread is lofty; add to this the flavor and one ends up with a unique epicurean treat.

Bread goes beyond being an edible; it is a metaphor for money, purity, peace, goodness and, in the Jewish tradition, is consumed with wine as a symbol of God providing what we need to survive.

There were plenty of Jewish bakeries in Buenos Aires where we could buy the *kuchen* that we split in the middle and filled with hot pastrami or other cold, cooked, cured or processed meats like salami and ham. Usually, we simply ate it during breakfast, spreading lots of butter on its flat side.

Time passed; for a long while the *bialy* disappeared from my life. I immigrated to the United States, worked as a physician in Pasadena, California, a mostly non-Jewish neighborhood, and finally retired to the West Side of Los Angeles, a mostly Jewish neighborhood, where, alas, I rediscovered the *bialy*. It was resuscitation, a rekindling of an old love.

In Los Angeles the bialy is easy to get, but not all are tasty; the shape is easy to imitate, its texture and taste very difficult.

Is the American *kuchelaj* superior to Saul's bialy? Of course not, but combining shape, flavor and imagination, some of them are as close to the *bialystocher kuchen* as they get.

And this is the beginning of the story.

The joy of warming up a *bialy* in the morning, that slowly starts radiating a smell of fresh bread and emanating a scent of onions became, for me a revered ritual. When I am away from home I embark in an expedition to find a good *kuchen*, a practice that became one of my hobbies. In New York I went to Kossar's, the famous and much praised bakery and had a tremendous disappointment. The roll was large, thick with burnt onions. Mimi Sheraton, a legendary food writer who has a passion for *bialys*, has described Kossar's as the place to get them. Perhaps after they underwent a change of ownership the quality vanished, and today they are not the treat that one may expect. In Miami I fetched them from different places, including Aventura, a Jewish enclave, to be met only by disappointment.

The *bialystocher kuchen (aka kuchelaj, aka bialy)* became for me a joyful distraction and then suddenly and unexpectedly I found an assignment that could take me to my ancestors - one that perhaps could answer many questions that I had lingering in my mind: Did my grandfather Moishe Mendl invent the *bialy*? Was he one of the best bakers in Bialystok? Were the ones made in Buenos Aires by my uncle Saul comparable to the ones he made in Bialystok? Why do *bialys* look different from place to place? I wanted to find the answers to these questions and after I received an invitation to go to Poland, that became my quest.

I gathered information from Mimi Sheraton's book *The Bialy Eaters,* which had a sub-narrative about Poland, the war and the Holocaust. She visited Bialystok, Buenos Aires, Paris and Israel, among others, in her expedition to rediscover the *bialy*. I learned, to my chagrin, that apparently it was not my grandfather (or perhaps he was) who conceived it. Its creation was attributed to a Moshe Nosovich, who had three bakeries (Moishe Mendl had two). In her pursuit, she learned that today, the *bialy* in Bialystok is practically unknown. In Paris people told her interesting stories about Bialystok, but there were none about the *kuchen.* Nor did she find them in Israel. In Buenos Aires she talked to several Bialystokers, ate at the Succot David, a kosher restaurant, and was told the same tales about Bialystok that I have heard from my family and friends.

Cut to 2011. My son calls me to invite me to go to Poland, where he was going to broadcast an international soccer game in Warsaw. "Poland, Dad - the land of your ancestors, the long-forgotten land that your parents swore they would never visit again. After the game we could go to Bialystok to trace your grandparents' bakeries and see if once and for all we can reclaim the honor of Moishe Mendl having been the creator of the kuchen."

I had mixed feelings: Poland was the country that my parents left because of pervasive anti-Semitism, the country involved in terrible pogroms, one that built infamous concentration camps, and where in 1971, long after the war ended, a bunch of villains destroyed the Bialystok ghetto cemetery on Zabia Street.

But Bialystok is also a city where for many years lived a thriving Jewish community, where prominent people like Albert Sabin, the developer of the polio vaccine; L.L. Zamenhof, the creator of Esperanto; and Max Weber, the painter, lived. Bialystok fosters a certain camaraderie and kinship among our ancestors.

Warsaw, our first stop, proved to be, to my surprise, a modern city restored after the war to its original form with the addition of modern buildings that followed a strict building code. The streets and avenues are well kept. The city has a mixture of architectural styles that does not detract from its beauty. There are many open, vast parks and monuments, museums, libraries and public spaces. Transportation is eased by a new Warsaw Metro.

Although it joined the European Union in 2004, it was able to avoid the ravages that the financial crisis of the last four years brought to most of the European countries, because it preserved its own currency.

The day after the soccer game, played in a newly constructed, beautiful stadium, we hired a guide to take us to Bialystok. The trip took about three hours; we were surprised to see hundreds of workers building new roads using state of the art machinery, an expression of a vibrant, ongoing economy.

We arrived in Bialystok at noon. I was expecting some emotional outbreak; to my surprise nothing happened. The center of the city, Osiedle Centrum, is unattractive and lined with simple stores and restaurants and not much green; the city is rather austere and grey. The main tourist attraction is Branicki's Palace which at one time belonged to the family of the same name that owned the entire city in the 18th century and who were protectors of the Jews. The population density is high and there are hundreds of people walking on the streets.

After a short visit it was time to start our search, which had three purposes: to locate my grandfather's bakery, the houses where my father and mother were born and visit some bakeries to learn about the *bialystoker kuchen.* We went to City Hall to retrieve information, were given huge registrars with the names of all inhabitants from

1880 to 1950 that did not produce any Kantors, much to our disappointment, and there were no bakeries bearing our name. Later, we strolled around the city and surprisingly, we did not find any bakeries; we asked at a restaurant and at markets that sold bread and pastries and were told that there were no local bakeries; products were only delivered to them from industrial confectionary and wholesale bakery manufacturers.

There were no *kuchen* in Bialystok and none of the people we talked to had any idea of its existence or recognized the name.

Happily, the *bialy*, bread like no other, is still alive and well in some parts of the world - just not in Poland.

Perhaps Moishe Mendl was not the one that invented it, but he was a masterful maker, responsible with few others for providing the world with a simple, distinctive bread roll, a feast to our palate that gives so much joy and pleasure to so many.

More importantly, he was among the few responsible for a tradition that is well and alive in the United States, a conversation piece, a link to a world long gone.

Ecstasy

Oh beautiful girl,

You asked me

To unrobe

And I did.

Then you came down;

My skin felt your skin

But you were in command,

With the strength

Of a staccato waltz

With all you have:

Your knuckles,

Your feet,

Your elbows,

Your hands…

How much pain,

How much pleasure

From you I got,

And then

You asked me

To open my legs,

To spread my arms,

To bend my knees,

And again

You came down.

I asked you,

"Not that rough,"

And you obliged.

I was in hell at times

Because of you,

Then

Your strokes

Your thumps -

I was in heaven at times;

Do you remember?

You jumped on me,

Stepped on me,

Stood on me -

The soothing music

Coming from somewhere.

How sweet of you!

You wrapped me

First with your hands,

Then a warm blanket

To cover

The land

That you brought back.

I feel so good,

So whole,

Intact -

By golly,

What a nice Thai Massage!

A love letter

This story is about my father Richard Denton, a man of pristine integrity, who conducted his life with honor and courage. He was born to riches; his grandfather owned six high rise buildings in the Chicago and New York areas and several shopping malls in different parts of the country. All these properties became part of our family trust and we, the descendants, enjoyed the fruits of those wise investments.

When each of his children reached 22 years of age, we were required to go through a ritual. We were sequestered in a room with a group of accountants and lawyers who would go over the assets that the family possessed, as we learned the history of the acquisitions, their value, and the real and projected income they generated. We were given a lesson on taxation, appreciation, depreciation, prospective gains, incumbent laws and all other paraphernalia related to our possessions. This intensive preparation would enable us to manage our wealth. Three months after this initial course the head of the law firm would meet with us for two purposes: one, to make sure that we had grasped all that we were supposed to know and second, to give us direction on how to conduct our business as the holders of such vast holdings. Later, those who were of age would become part of the family board.

We were extremely rich, and the fluctuations of the national or international economy would not make a dent in our capital. There was no way that something could affect our prosperity. Overseeing the managers, our only duty, was after a while an easy task. We didn't have to work for our subsistence, only watch over our interests.

We accepted our wealth as fate with dignity and humility. During our family reunions we never talked about money; opulence and affluence were not part of our vocabulary. In spite of living in a different space from those who earned their money with effort and sweat, we were not arrogant. We inherited the decorum of our ancestors, who built their fortunes with strength and pride.

In spite of, or because of, our fortune, we were not allowed to stay idle. My parents were well aware of the fate of many who had come to wealth, like us, who would end their lives with boredom, addiction, vagrancy and suicide. They made sure that we all got a superior education and were provided a thorough knowledge of politics, geography, history, art and philosophy.

We were descendants of Ulysses Grant and were prepared to praise or defend him in every context.

When we finished college, my mother made us become involved in different Foundations. I chose Grintao, an organization dedicated to preserving animals on the verge of extinction. At the beginning it was only a distraction; then I learned how scavengers killed creatures from the animal kingdom without mercy to make a profit, at which time I decided to put my best skills to work in the enterprise.

My dad was an educated man; he received a Master in Political Philosophy from Princeton University. He was an avid, incessant booklover with the gift of an extraordinary memory that allowed him to quote the essentials of his readings. He would cite a phrase or a statement from an author when it fitted a situation. When a politician was being convicted of a crime, he would quote Machiavelli's *'politics have no relation to morals'*; when my sister fell in love with a man of a different faith than ours, dad quoted Einstein: *'gravitation is not responsible for people falling in love'*. And the one that applied to us (did he make it up?): *'don't rejoice about your wealth, you don't know where the journey may take you'*.

He was a devout Catholic and inculcated the love of God to his five children.

Dad married his college sweetheart Ann, a patrician lady of immense beauty. Mother was quiet and humble. She dedicated her life to her family and to her charities. She founded *Intelligent Giving,* an institution that provides funds for education to underserved children. This charitable organization spends only three percent of its revenue in administrative costs, and was recognized in Fortune Magazine as the best managed of its kind.

Ours was a happy family. At home there was a never-ending background noise of laughter, ceaseless chatting and an energy emerging from my four younger sisters.

The family chores that my parents had were unremitting: there was always a toddler to take care of; when one got a cold the rest us felt obliged to 'share' it; the task of going to kindergarten or school demanded that we get up at 6 o'clock every morning.

My sister Maria, one year younger than I, was lovable and wild. She became the leader of the pack; she was joyful, witty, and strong, with an unbreakable will; a protector of her siblings, a role that I should have assumed but did not. Martha, Pauline and Theresa were happy toddlers and then became happy women.

The home entourage was completed by Betsy and Malcolm, a married couple that lived in the downstairs quarters. She was the housekeeper and he the driver, who also fulfilled other tasks. Their two daughters Clarisse and Patty were our occasional sitters, but did not live on the premises.

Life for us was good. We were a gang, a delicious crowd interested in having as much fun as possible without breaking the austere norms imposed by our parents. Going to school was amusing and enjoyable, and for many years it was made easy by dad who was actively engaged with our education, an undertaking that he enjoyed utilizing unorthodox and original means.

There was a large world map in his office and from it, we played the games that he developed as a learning tool. *Nigeria was located in West Africa, populated by three ethnic groups, near the Atlantic; they were colonized by the British*. This was followed by an explanation as how the different empires colonized the land of others and how they reacted to the impositions of the foreigners who were occupying their land. Dad's questions were incessant, until he was convinced that the answers became ingrained in us. He would not accept recitation of facts without an understanding of their meaning. This type of education was better than the narrations demanded in our schools. Those encounters with our father were unforgettable. We understood the world in its different dimensions at an early stage of our lives.

My best friend was Ahmed, the son of the Yemen Ambassador to the US. I surprised him when I asked if he was born in Yemen's capital Sana'a. I was the first American he met that knew this piece of geography. When I told him that one day I wanted to go to the Island of Socotra to visit the limestone caves, our friendship was cemented forever.

One summer, when I was 14 years old, my parents told us that we were going to take a trip and that we, the kids, were going to decide where. We were given the task to go to Dad's library and use his books and maps to decide a place. Maria took charge of the enterprise: first we needed to choose a country and then a city. I wanted to go to China; Maria to Australia; Martha to Italy, Pauline to France, and little Theresa was too young to have an opinion. The discussion became heated; I learned that all my sisters were opinionated and had an enviable sense of determination. We were five vivacious children, all with strong and different personalities. Our parents taught us well. We ended up going to Australia – oh Maria! Before taking the trip we became acquainted with the country from Sarah Helman's Australia ABC. Our parents were proud of our erudition: we knew everything about the Tasmanian Sea, the Great Barrier Reef and Australian geography and history, which made the trip enjoyable.

I was happy to be the second man in the family. I felt, perhaps unfoundedly, that I had a strong bond with dad, perhaps related to our manhood; a feeling, grounded on emotion more than reason.

I have hundreds of memories of our family life that never fade and marked me as the man I am.

One time, while we were having dinner, I was disrespectful to Betsy because she did not acquiesce to something I asked her. Afterwards Dad called me to his office and scolded me for my behavior and then gave me a lesson on equality, respect and civility.

On another occasion I was playing tennis with a friend in our summer home and my parents were watching. I called a ball out which was likely in; later Dad lectured me about cheating and deceiving and told me that when there is a doubt one should concede.

The example of how he lived his life - his measured devotion to God, his humanistic qualities and his sense of duty to the less unfortunate people - made me admire the man, the gentle man that my father was. He had a sweet demeanor, a gentle face, and a keen sense of humor. He had an ability to tell and concoct stories that reminded me of William Buckley. He had a tender emotional streak, which showed in the way he caressed my mother and hugged my sisters and me.

My best encounters were always in his library; Dad would ask me about my assignments in class and derived from them some consequential conversations. When I was assigned to discuss *A Christmas Carol* by Charles Dickens, he asked me to recount what I read, which I did mechanically, without a true understanding of the narrative. Dad explained how Scrooge represented the conflict that Dickens had with his father, who had been imprisoned for a short time, and how the plot reflects joy and misery, death in one part and renewal of life in another. I read the book again and for the first time understood how meaningful it was. From then on, it was easy for me to discover the genius of writers. Memorizing became the foe of knowledge. Comprehension was discernment and without it, information was useless.

One day Father summoned the family to tell us that the President had offered him a position in his cabinet as a special advisor. He had known Dad since college, knew of his intellectual acumen and his capacity to resolve problems. Dad had been the President of the Student Council at Princeton and in that function he resolved many difficult problems.

They remained friends after college. One time, the President called him because he was facing a difficult dilemma. He was running for reelection; the polls showed a virtual tie with his opponent. Four weeks before Election Day, his wife was found to have a brain tumor. This created a quandary. He was afraid that announcing her problem to the country was going to be seen as political opportunism. His election strategists' opinions were divided; withholding information would be a breach of confidence with the electorate but the opposite could be seen as taking advantage of a dire situation: he could be labeled as devious, and unprincipled. Father advised him to communicate to the public that the First Lady was undergoing tests for a condition that was affecting her, she was resting comfortably (which was true) and the results of her medical tests would be announced a few days after the election. He requested the public to respect the privacy of his wife; they would inform the people of any unexpected occurrence. The President was reelected and asked Dad to become part of his cabinet as a special advisor.

Dad discussed the pros and cons of moving to Washington. To serve the country was a great honor and a challenge, but it would represent a huge change in his life. Working in the White House would take him away from his family. There was not much debate; it was easy for all of us to appreciate the honor of serving the President.

The entire family became active in helping with the move to Washington. Mother was in charge of the overall strategy; Pauline fetched the new habitat for Dad, Maria bought all the furniture for the new home, and I became in charge of setting up all the computers, the Wi Fi and other chores. By doing so we all became part of the enterprise. He was to live in an apartment in Georgetown, big enough to accommodate us during our visits. He was to commute back home as frequently as possible, probably four or five times a year.

What a commotion! Mother organized a celebratory party; that day became the proudest moment for our family.

His sporadic visits to our home were pure joy and delight.

We were thrilled and vain when Dad was interviewed on television. He was a frequent guest on CNN and MSNBC. Once he spent a full hour with Bill Moyers discussing poverty in the third world, a subject that was dear to his heart. He made bold proposals about how the U.N. could end hunger in the world, engaging a Commission of notables that would include 10 people from France, China, Russia, South Africa, Italy, Uruguay and the United States. This interview made the front page of the New York Times. The project took off; then he became busier than ever, having three important chores: take care of his finances – an easy task; advising the president – not such an easy job; and working on the Poverty Project – an extremely difficult endeavor.

I was determined to follow his colossal steps; I knew deep in my heart that it was going to be a venture of gargantuan proportions.

In high school I had a group of very good friends, who made my life whole. Sebastian was a great quarterback on our football team and was already recruited by the University of Michigan with a full scholarship; Dwight was handsome, somewhat petulant but sensitive and caring. He had high aspirations and wanted to be a Senator like his dad; Francis was a free spirit with a passion for cooking, determined to open a restaurant after finishing college. With them we discussed menial and meaningful subjects like religion (Francis was agnostic), politics, sports and of course, girls. We played electronic games constantly - the sports video games were invariably won by Francis, Sebastian always won the swimming races and Dwight prevailed in discussions about history.

I don't know how to define happiness other than being the opposite of not being happy. Going to school was a jolly experience, being with my family was a delight, reading and playing was a gleeful experience; I was surrounded by a happy bunch of people.

Then, abruptly with no warning, an uninvited provocation - Fate? Destiny? Serendipity? Providence? - came to take the joy of life from my family, to interrupt what appeared to be uninterruptable, to halt everything I cherished.

Announced just by a knock on the door: "We are so sorry," said one of the two policemen, "Mr. Richard Denton's car skidded on the icy road and the vehicle flipped. Mr. Denton had an accident with his car, somehow the air bag did not inflate, he hit his head on the windshield and died instantly. He was only 12 miles from your home."

Was there anything we could do to bring him back? Could we stop his departure?

This was unimaginable, unreal, abstruse!

My mother's husband was gone, Dad was gone, Mr. Denton was gone, the advisor for the President was gone, and there was no coming back. The futility and cruelty of death presented to us for the first time.

During the service he was praised by the President, his best friends, our priest and others. He was respected and admired, and yet all those reverences meant nothing to me. The only thing that really mattered was that he was gone forever.

Father Gabriel rendered the eulogy: "The Lord decided to take him for reasons only known to Him; there is no evil design; Richard is going to rest in peace and be accepted in heaven as the man he was on Earth. The land of the living has lost a good man, the land of the death gained an incomparable soul; he is being escorted by angels who will take him to an eternal rest. Life is always ephemeral, in his case shorter than we wished. Perhaps death is a metaphor because it is the precursor of the Other Life as God intended."

Bullshit, bullshit, bullshit, Father Gabriel, use your powers to resurrect my father. You always talk in your pulpit about the final resurrection. Dad is ready for his revivification; he was a man of good thoughts and good deeds. You taught us about the resurrection of the righteous. Paul said, "If there is no resurrection of the dead, then not even Christ has been raised." *Well then, bring him back.*

I don't know where God, my God, his God was when he had the accident.

My life changed forever, in a way that I did not expect and never considered. My sisters continued with their education. They got over the grief in their own way. Theresa and Pauline appeared happy again after less than one year; Martha and especially Maria showed their sorrow and the scars from Dad's absence until they got married and had their own children. Their kids gave them the renovation of life that they were looking for and little by little, their angst disappeared.

I could not come to terms with what happened; I needed an answer. Death is always unkind. For the first time the death of others became meaningful to me.

I felt in my bones the pain of helplessness. If I could find an explanation for suffering, for the demise of little children killed by cholera, or the fatal fate of women, children and civilians from bombs thrown from the skies by drones, or suicide bombers, or for those who died of malnutrition, only then I could explain the tragedy of my father's death.

The answer would have to come from God. Why did he deprive our family and the world of a man that was going to provide wellness to so many?

I could endure my pain if I could only understand.

Perhaps if there was no God I wouldn't need any answers: trees die, flowers die, animals die and humans die. There is a biological reason for that, so I don't need God any longer. Or do I?

There was only one way that I could end my torment. I locked myself with God in a world of meditation while at the same time I was going to help others. My solace was in the church, the one that advocates taking care of the needy, ending all wars, protecting the life of the unborn. I wanted to reclaim the life of my father, and I would do that by extending the teachings of God.

So I entered my congregation as part of its hierarchy, engaged in vivid discussions with Father John about the survival of the soul in a space known only to the Lord. I was preoccupied by our salvation and the forbidden salvation of others that did not belong to our faith, an incoherence I found in sacred texts. I exhorted him to share with me his thoughts about the afterlife. I needed to know how the righteous could prevail over evil, why virtue has an ever-changing dimension, how prayers work, why we condemned the non-baptized and why punishment of the damned can be accepted as part of our Doctrine.

Nothing from our discussions gave me comfort or consolation.

As time went by I replaced my existential uncertainties with action. I traveled all over the world to help the hungry, assist the destitute, lend a hand to the victims of natural disasters, and alleviate the poor from their miseries. The struggle to relieve poverty and suffering became my *raison de etre.*

The day I turned 28 years old I received a visit from the police. I dreaded unannounced visits. They came to inform me that as the Police Precinct was moving to a different place they found a briefcase that was in the trunk of my father's car the day of the accident and was stored in the basement of the police station and somehow remained there for all those years.

The images of the accident came back to me.

I could not open his attaché for many months. I was frightened that it might contain something that I did not want to see or know. One day, I became agitated and realized that I had to overcome my fretfulness. Inside the briefcase there were some official documents from the government, a book and a letter:

My dearest,

As I contemplate from my window the fallen snow I cannot stop my tears, thinking that I won't be seeing you for another ten days. I miss you so much already. I don't know why, but today I yearn for you as never before.

My life became whole the day I met you, your love has filled me with a plenitude that I never experienced. The images of our togetherness never leave me; I remember what we ate during our first lunch together, how you were dressed, and the words that you uttered so softly; I remember the moment I felt in love with you. From that day on I was agitated by the thrilling anticipation of our encounters. I did not want anything from you; your presence was enough to produce in me an immeasurable thrill.

One unexpected day you touched my hand, caressed my cheek and it was then that I knew that we shared the same feelings.

I never experienced a crushing desire until I met you; I never expected to have a friend, a companion, a lover that would arouse in me so much affection and so much longing.

Before knowing you, I was happy, my work was fulfilling, my relationships enjoyable and did not need much more in my life until I met you and realized what happiness truly is.

The bliss to touch you, to kiss you, to embrace you is what made my life whole for the very first time. I find joy in the exhilaration that your presence brings and in the delight of your company.

When our nude bodies become entangled I experience an ecstasy like never before and don't want to let it go. I touch your skin and it becomes my skin, when we make love and you look at me I feel an uncontrollable excitement that I wish could last forever.

When you are by my side, a dark day becomes radiant.

Richard, I know that our relationship has caused you delight and also concern. You now have to travel a road full of hurdles.

You have been asking yourself if there can be any morality in our sins, and I have been asking myself if there is any immorality in our love which is so intense, pure and celestial.

My dear, I will be no impediment to whatever action you may want to take. I know how important family, honor and virtue are for you. Nothing will change what I feel for you; my love is unconditional, total and eternal.

Do what you believe you need to do; I will accept your decision.

I will live with you for the rest of my life and live with the memories of these last two years.

When you are not by my side I still can see the splendor of your smile, hear the cadence of your voice - you may not be here but you are always with me.

Love of my life, be well

I adore you.

Marissa

It took me but a few seconds to understand.

The letter helped me to recognize the world as it is; life and death are sustained by love and they are unpredictable. My search was over.

Hindu Philosophy
The Sharing Stone

Hinduism is a set of beliefs that encompasses many philosophical points of view; through meditation, logic, praxis and knowledge it helps people achieve emotional stability and avoid perverted actions; to the believers it offers salvation and to the agnostics the promise of a happy life. For others is a source of creativity and gives the opportunity to reach otherwise unreachable aspirations.

From their nine schools of thought in the Hindu philosophy, there is one that has not been invented and I, Jaimini Bhatia, am proposing to correct some of the ills of civilization.

I have tried this objective in 24 persons, 12 males and 12 females, between 32 and 40 years of age.

I am a conceptual thinker. I use my own aphorisms to make the bottom line of my thoughts easy to grasp.

There are 200 members in my Beverly Hills congregation.

I applied this new experiment exactly one year ago.

During a first memorable session, I brought 24 flat stones of iridescent colors of about four inches in size. I explained that Perfect Harmony could be achieved by applying the stone between the temples of two persons and listening to soothing music which was to be provided by an iPod. The sessions would last three hours and would be repeated four times. The participants, through enhanced meditation, would achieve spiritual discernment, physical purification, a path for finding their own God and a peaceful existence.

The cost of the stone and seminar was 1.2 million dollars per person. As a bonus, I provided the iPod with the pre-programmed music for free.

Twenty-four persons signed up to become part of the first trial without hesitation, and 22 others were placed on a waiting list.

After I collected 28.8 million dollars we were ready for the encounter.

We may have been blessed by God because during the five days that the experiment lasted, the weather was perfect.

I rented a large recreational area in Stone Canyon Park and summoned the partakers to arrive promptly at 6 o'clock in the morning.

It was magnificent to observe them arriving in their Lamborghinis, Ferraris, Mercedes and Rolls Royce's. Sharon, though, arrived in an old Lexus, since in order to pay her tuition she sold her Bentley and refinanced her home.

The sessions consisted of one person applying the stone gently on the right of his/her temple and the other on the left temple and share the flow of knowledge that would come through the stone. They would be embedded by the music from the iPod but to avoid distraction, they were to give complete attention to their thoughts.

The sessions were completed by the end of the week. The members were radiant and happy and departed from the facility with big smiles on their faces.

The results of Perfect Harmony will be published in a book, which most likely will become a best seller since my publisher is one of the more aggressive, unethical and astute persons that I ever met.

In my appreciation the events have been absolutely therapeutic for all 24 persons. Succinctly, these are the conclusions that I reached after those five days:

1. Having a lot of money does not make a person wise.

2. People are gullible.

3. The power of seduction is strong.

4. The force of suggestibility is infinite.

5. Those who realized what happened to their 1.2 million dollars became humble and self-effacing; achievements which are difficult to emulate with any other therapeutic technique.

6. Myths and deceptions are here to stay.

7. A flat, small, beautiful iridescent stone is a nice and effective placebo.

8. Peace, calm and happiness is in the eyes of the beholder.

9. Everything is relative.

One additional note (which I will elaborate in the soon to be published book): Michael Heinz told me that after the Sharing Stone workshop, his repressed creativity came back and he wrote a movie script which became a big success; he is currently nominated for an Oscar.

Unfortunately, the Lexus lady lost her home from her inability to pay the mortgage. She is now working as a paralegal and saving money to participate in one of our future meetings.

I still live in the same house in Bel Air that is being remodeled and traded my Volkswagen for a Porsche, which I will return because the engine is very noisy.

Those who are interested in signing up for one of my Seminars, please write me at: sharingthebrilliantstone@gmail.com

THE GOLD MEDAL

When they entered, they found hanging upon the wall a splendid portrait of their master as they had last seen him, in all the wonder of his exquisite youth and beauty. Lying on the floor was a dead man, in evening dress, with a knife in his heart. He was withered, wrinkled, and loathsome of visage. it was not till they had examined the rings that they recognized who it was. (The Portrait of Dorian Grey - Oscar Wilde)

He was a determined young man; at age 16 he decided to become a physician. He despised his father's profession, although he loved him deeply. It was not in his makeup to follow his steps and be a tailor; perhaps he should use his sewing skills that he learned as a child and become a surgeon.

He was one of our 'gang' of four. At the beginning of our last year in college, we decided to apply to Medical School. Fifty years ago the choice of profession for middle class boys appeared to be few: lawyer, physician, architect, engineer or dentist. All others were 'exotic'. The schoolmates that applied to humanistic professions were the weirdoes.

The ones that were gifted with an artistic vein were the exception.

In other cases, strong, traditional families dictated the path to their children. Landowners sent them to Business Schools to learn how to preserve or increase the family wealth. Large, Catholic, well-to-do families had one son in the clergy and one in the military.

Mordechai, from the beginning, was determined to obtain the Gold Medal Award in Medical School. This was awarded to the best student of his class, a difficult, almost impossible task for us, but not for Mordy, as we called him, who was endowed with a high IQ, a vivid imagination, strength of mind and an unbreakable willpower.

The Award is the equivalent of graduating Summa Cum Laude - with the highest honor - a level of distinction that in our Medical School was awarded to only one individual. Our professors knew that Mordechai and Willie were competing for the honor and sadistically squeezed them to their deep viscera during finals.

Mordy got a grade point average of 9.8 and Willie 9.69.

Mordechai kept The Gold Medal in a glass case. His achievement reached thousands of people - those who count - by word of mouth.

This simple 2 by 2 inches, piece of yellow, non-corrosive, shiny metallic element opened the doors for Mordy: Yale, Baylor and Oxford.

He gained a well-deserved reputation; he was as knowledgeable as innovative. He simplified surgical techniques and invented new ones. At the age of 32 he founded a Cardiovascular Institute that until today bears his name, where he worked until his retirement.

His academic achievements were coupled with enormous wealth.

He was given twelve Scientific Awards during the 50 years of his career, but none had the symbolism or the role that the Gold Medal had, which by itself reflected Mordechai's sense of purpose in life.

Mordy and his wife Sarah, his biggest supporter and cheerleader, had a happy life. As time passed by they enjoyed each other more and more.

After many years, I reencountered Mordy again in New York. It was pure serendipity. We both were staying at the Plaza Hotel. One day as I was having an afternoon tea with my wife, I recognized him immediately. Although he had aged, he remained the Mordy I knew. I, on the other hand, although fit, had become bald; physically I was a different man from who I used to be.

We renewed our friendship and became acquainted with our respective families.

We played chess at his home, as we used to during our youth. The living room of his home was masterfully decorated with a mixture of modern and classical style. The ornaments reflected the remembrance of their trips around the world. The colors of the rooms and the soothing lights added to the joy of our game.

The Gold Medal was displayed in an oak cabinet, standing proudly all alone and guarded by a clear, thick glass.

Then, something very surprising happened. For the very first time I started winning game after game, exactly the opposite experience from years past. One day, Mordy was telling me about his achievements as editor of a prestigious scientific journal but could not remember its name. Sarah confided to me that Mordy was becoming progressively forgetful.

After few months he reached the edge of his life.

At the same time, the Gold Medal in the glass case became corroded, lost its luster, color and ductility. Its glow of sunrise was gone forever.

A New Word for a New World

My name is Alexander Constantinescu. I was born in Timisoara, Western Romania, in 1980.

Romanian is a Romance language like French, Italian, Catalan, Spanish and Portuguese, which explains why I was able to master many languages. I also speak French, Spanish and Italian fluently; this gave me prestige and a remarkable social advantage. I immigrated to the United States in 1994 and mastered English, which became my most common form of expression in less than one year. I speak all of them almost without an accent. Only the lack of certain idioms makes people aware that I may not be a native.

I love idiomatic expressions; they are tricky, ingenuous and funny. I learned the meaning of *to pay through the nose* years ago when I paid 35 dollars for one hour parking in New York; *in bocca al lupo (into the wolf's mouth)* in Italy is used to mean 'good luck', which exceeds my understanding; *a toda maquina,* literally *at all machine* in Spanish, means quickly, simple and graphic.

Today I am able to use almost most of them as an indigenous person. It is fun and an interesting intellectual exercise.

After finishing college I became an expert in the field of linguistics; this discipline became my passion. Not only I was interested in the traditional role of linguistics in studying meaning and structure of words but also in the cultural and social meaning of verbal communication and the interplay with nonverbal forms of expression. Pitch, volume and intonation, either with sounds or words, became my field of expertise; this aspect of languages has been explored by me and others; it is a subject that I discussed in different public forums to enlighten different audiences: historians, politicians, novelists, and others.

I am skilled in phonetics and have published what today is considered the definitive paper in psycholinguistics: *"The perception of speech sound as a manifestation of deranged emotions"*.

My knowledge in this field has allowed me to advance in the understanding of other disciplines like philosophy, anthropology, computer science and psychology, which gravitated in my comprehension of the human being.

Freedom of speech is a throne and censorship the oven that villains use to destroy ideas. I always defend the right to speak your mind and condemn the absurdity of trying to suppress any form of communication, no matter its content.

I am also an inventor, holding 122 patents. More than half of my creations are currently in the market. Some of them are improvements upon established products, while others are original creations. I am convinced that there is a correlation between my linguistic skills and my creativity, which made me inquisitive about the meaning of things; from there, the path to conceive new things is short.

I invented an air conditioner that has a compressor two-thirds smaller than the standard ones while it has twice the cooling capacity of conventional ones. In addition its shape, design and color have changed the architectural face of millions and millions of buildings where the old, large boxy apparatus has been replaced by the one that I devised, which is definitely original and inconspicuous.

A low-cost sun-powered hybrid car, developed entirely by my group of engineers, will be presented to the public at the end of this year.

An app which allows for the pages of any electronic book to turn upon eye command is already being tested and is working better than expected.

I am an achiever with a social consciousness and had make the products of my creation accessible to the public. In spite of all these accomplishments I found that something was absent from my life. I wanted to make a cultural contribution to the world.

One day, out of nowhere, I realized that I could create a conceptual universal metaphor in the shape of one single word.

The conception was bold, simple, useful, practical and wise - one that brought me ecstasy and delight. I already have fame and money - fame which I did not seek and money that I do not need. I wanted a feeling of realization exceeding what other accomplishments had brought me.

Through this one accomplishment I became happy and whole.

I invented one word which could be used indistinctively as a noun, an adjective, an adverb and a verb. This word has no structure and syntaxes do not apply. It is free of constraints and orthography becomes irrelevant. It has a built-in semantic, is pragmatic and can be used every day as a form of communication.

The word is *biloin* and it means whatever you want it to mean. It can mean good or bad, decent or indecent, enjoyable or boring, work or play, tall or short and everything else. A word, that for the first time, means what the context dictates and not what conventional linguistics wants to represent. *Biloin* can be used in any language and retain its purpose. It is harmonious and easy to synchronize with any form of communication, either oral or written. It is easy to pronounce in any of the 6800 distinct languages of the world.

The concept is so revolutionary that at the beginning, it may be difficult to grasp the beauty of its use.

According to my calculations, it will take two years for the word to become universal.

Several examples will remove the obstacles from the forest and will make clear what it can achieve:

You go to see a movie. After the show, as is customary, you and your wife like to discuss the script, actors and all other aspects of the film. In the past, your comments and analysis were thorough and long. Now it is different. As you are stepping out from the theatre, she tells you, "What a biloin!" That is it; no more is needed. The word has clearly delivered her opinion. No need to expand further.

You are riding in your car with your wife and your two teenager kids, a girl and a boy. You are a typical Christian family that knows very well the boundaries of social rules. You are observant of good norms and know to restrain and not express your feelings if they are inconvenient to others. This is a long trip from Burbank to Fresno. Suddenly there is a smell in the car - a bad smell, one that you do not appreciate. You would not dare

86

to utter what would be perhaps common with other families: "Who farted?" Your moral constraints are such that you deem it better to keep the unpleasant sensation to yourself and don't say anything. But there is another way that can do several things simultaneously. You can say, "Who biloin?" and everybody would understand, the perpetrator would feel guilty and refrain from doing it again. You will be at peace with your soul. Your family will see you as the keeper of good manners. You save the day.

Elaine is summoned by Christopher, the head of a Goldman Sachs Division. She has been working for the firm for nine years. She has a salary of $140,000 a year plus a variable bonus. Chris tells her that their global investments are going sour and the Company is forced to trim personnel. She is being fired and asked to leave immediately; she is going to be escorted to the parking lot by Timothy, a junior associate. Elaine is a fast thinker, witty and smart. In a few seconds of reflection, she renounces doing or saying what she wants and feels; she may need a letter of recommendation from them to secure another job. She experiences an intense internal turmoil. She feels like picking the sharp letter opener that is on the desk and stabbing Christopher in his face - his eyes, more specifically. It is either that or say nothing and leave the room, frustrated by restraining her emotions. There is a third alternative, which will clearly do two things for her: let her keep her *sanity and be true to herself. So clearly and loudly she says, "Chris, go and biloin yourself!"*

Other very brief instances which would explain the worth of my new word:

Contemplating the sunset in the Pacific: "What a biloin!"

Lost while driving: "Where the biloin are we?"

"Honey would you like to biloin tonight?"

Now, don't dismiss my idea so fast! The new utterance may also temper things that are bad and enhance many that are good. If a person is about to be evicted from his/her house after falling behind in the rent, receiving an expulsion notice can be devastating; if instead the notification reads *"You are being biloin,"* the person will have time to pause for few minutes to try to figure out what it really means. This will slow their mental process and consequently the emotional devastation.

If there is an earthquake in Guatemala the news to all will be better served with something like *"Biloin rattles Guatemala."*

If a high ranking, decorated, well-respected, admired, praised Army General is caught cheating on his wife, exchanging amorous e-mails with his lover and carrying on an affair for years; there are two alternatives: announcing the event in the media with expletives will harm all involved parties, place the prestige of the Armed Forces in question, threaten national security and disappoint millions of followers. The words <u>affair</u> and <u>scandal</u> bring indignity, humiliation and dishonor to many. Instead, using *biloin* as the descriptive makes the whole thing to a level of tittle-tattle which would be easier to absorb: 'General Stoneus admits a *biloin* with his biographer'. This places the General in the context of somebody that has the *biloin* to confront the truth and make everybody understand that *biloin* is part of human nature.

The word will be easy to appreciate in every context; if the Stock Market goes up: *The Dow reached new biloin*, and if it goes down *The Dow fell to a new biloin.*

The word may become interchangeable in every language, which will make the understanding between civilizations more fluid. In France *Bon biloin* will be good for good morning, afternoon and evening. In Italy *biloin* with marinara sauce is clearly spaghetti or pappardelle; in Spain *biloin* in the context of a dance is clearly flamenco; in Russia no more Comrade - from now on it will be *Biloin Lenin or Biloin Stalin*, which will prevent us from evoke the dark era of Communism.

The fish merchant won't have to spend money with costly signs in their shop announcing *'We sell Fresh Fish'* - after all, people know that he wouldn't give away his merchandise, or believe that the fish is rotten and not fresh, and of course the smell will be sufficient to preclude naming what they sell.

Therefore one word only may replace four: "*Biloin*", an economical and creative way to advertise his products.

Time will tell if my contribution may endure the passage of time. I *biloin* so.

A Story of Love and other Coincidences

We were having a serious conversation. I don't remember why I brought up the subject, perhaps from a need of reassurance that everything in my life was all right. I was telling Rebecca, my sister, that we were lucky to have been raised in a 'normal' family. Our parents had been married for 29 years, they had a good relationship; they did have two crises that we knew of, but they resolved, we thought, because they truly loved each other. We were raised in a calm environment; there were some, but not many, arguments among us. Although Mom was a disciplinarian we had freedom to become what we wanted to be. I felt that Dad loved me a little bit more than he loved my sister and Mammy was more tolerant and effusive with Rebecca. Perhaps unfounded perceptions; but the fact was that we felt that the four of us owned each other. We protected each other ferociously; we knew about our whereabouts all the time; we shared pain and laughter. "Look Gaby," Sis said, "how many people we know that were raised in dysfunctional families. Our cousin Theodore is into drugs and alcohol; his sister has already been divorced twice; our friend Eloisa has been dishonored by her parents because she married a Jew; Angelina Jolie had a horrible relation with her dad and so many others like them. I think we were lucky, or is dysfunctional the new normal?

As I was about to interject my thoughts I felt a jolt on my leg. It hurt. I looked around to learn what exactly happened - where was this coming from, by heavens! - and then I saw a young man whose face gradually turned white. He approached us; he was contrite and apologetic. In spite of the scratch and pain on my limb I could not help but feel sorry for him. He looked at the leg and noticed that there was no big harm. We were near La Maison du Chocolat, so he insisted for us to go there and sit down. His name was Gabby, short for Gabrielle. We laughed about the fluke of having the same name. There was no six degrees of separation, he said with some humor, just a b. Gradually, he became his own self. Gabby explained that he was walking and saw an object on the sidewalk, which he instinctively kicked, without looking around. It was the stone that landed on my leg. We spent twenty minutes chatting; suddenly we locked eyes and I realized that I was hooked. Blissfully, he asked if he could see me again. We exchanged phone numbers and noticed that the last four digits were the same as mine. Again we laughed.

When he left Rebecca proclaimed, "It is fate; he is the one for you."

She was right; Gabby, who I nicknamed Stone, became the love of my life. First I was attracted to his looks, his angular jaw, and penetrating gaze from his dark eyes and then, slowly I discovered his grace, his intelligence, and became enamored of his personality. He was a happy, easygoing chap, always smiling. Gabrielle 'Stone' McPierson did not have to worry much about the needs of existence. He was the heir to the Litty Department Stores, founded by his grandfather, which went public in the 70s and had its shares climbing to unanticipated heights over the last 10 years.

Gabby founded with Raul, his gay best friend, the son of the owner of a Spanish television network, a Charitable Foundation to prevent malnutrition in underdeveloped countries. Gabby's devotion to help others became his raison d'être. It was amazing to see how creative thinking and their astuteness made the Foundation one of the most efficient institutions in the world.

He was a sportsman, played polo, tennis and was an avid surfer. Raul always joked that after him his friend was the best surfer in the planet.

Gabby and I became lovers; I always teased him by telling him that his caresses made me feel like I had two G spots (pun intended).

One rainy day we decided to stay home. Stone cooked his specialty, eggplant parmigiana (the only thing he knew how to cook), and we drank one full bottle of Lucatta, his favorite wine. We were happy and merry; life was fun.

In the background, the TV was playing a commercial from eHarmony. I jokingly proposed Stone to take a compatibility test, to see if we matched. We accessed their website. The results were surprising: we both were leaders, and we asked ourselves if that was good or dire for the relationship. He was adventurous and I was not. I was more reflexive than he was; he was kinder than I was. He was more extroverted, less dominant, more social, less inquisitive, and more ambitious. Then Gabby said, "I may not know if we are compatible but there is one thing I am certain of: I adore you and want to worship you for the rest of my life. I want to raise a family with you; would you marry me?"

That night we made love again and again. It was ecstasy, it was joy, it was happiness.

The next day I called Rebecca and told her the news and asked her to help me with the logistics. She was a corporate executive at Neiman Marcus and knew how to plan. Since I was working as a Literature Professor at NYU, we decided to set up the wedding for December, during my Christmas vacation break. Gabby proposed to take a short vacation in Portugal in July, spend a week and explore places for our honeymoon.

We flew to Lisbon; from the airport we rented a car and took the ferry straight to Peniche, a delightful fishing town with sandy beaches, a magical place with spectacular grottoes and picturesque rocky formations. We stayed at Longorio's, a charming Bed and Breakfast. 'Stone' surfed during the day and we had dinner every night at 9.30, Portugal style. We made a lot of acquaintances from the local surfing community, all easygoing, tanned youngsters, who apparently never worked one day in their life.

On July 24, Gabby went surfing with a small group of his new friends. I stayed in the lodge to prepare a dissertation at the University.

At noon the owner of the B&B summoned me to the living room. There, three gloomy adolescents were crying inconsolably. They told me the terrible news. Gabby was riding on his surfboard and became trapped in a large wave; his ankle was attached to a leash and what was supposed to protect him was the cause of his demise, dragging him under the water. He drowned and in spite of the efforts of these kids to resuscitate him, he never came back. I was petrified, could not shed a tear nor utter a word. I cried for days and days, for nights and nights.

Rebecca, her boyfriend Spencer and Raul flew to Lisbon and made all the arrangements to take Gabby back to the US.

The burial remains a shadowy scene. I don't remember much, only that I woke up several weeks later from this nightmare. For the first time in my life I was confronted with issues of death, grief, and the meaning of existence; this forced me to recalibrate my life. Before Gabby's demise my life was flowing freely, with preoccupation about my career and my relationship with him, and not much more.

Life was now Before Gabby and After Gabby.

Time passed. I did not get back to normal - whatever that means - for a long time. After a year Rebecca encouraged me to start dating again, which I did, trying to be sensible and pragmatic. I knew that life could not end there and yet I continued with a sense of nothingness. All my readings to prepare my classes at NYU deviated in my mind into questions of death and dying. Hemingway became relevant because he wrote *The Fifth Column* while Madrid was being bombarded, Faulkner because of "As I Lay Dying". My focus reading newspapers was on young soldiers dying needlessly in stupid wars.

One day, out of the blue, I felt an urge. I wanted to be a mother - not a wife, a mother. The thought of having a baby gave me a glow that I had not experienced since Gabby was alive. I had a new mission and I threw myself into it with passion and contentment. I was exultant from anticipation.

I called Rebecca; she noticed right away that something important was happening to me. I told her that we were going to discuss it over lunch at The Grill.

"Gaby, I have not seen you so cheerful for quite some time, what is going on?"

"I want to have a baby!"

"You met somebody!!!? I am so happy for you! Who is he; do I know him?"

"I said that I want to have a baby, not that I met somebody. I felt an inner blaze and didn't know what it was, until I realized that. The desire is here and is real. I am not selfish; I will not bring the baby to distract me, to fill a void. I will love, nurture, raise and cherish him or her. I feel that I don't have to understand or explain why I feel this way, but I know that this is going to be good for me and the baby."

"But you are aware," she said, laughing, "that you need a partner unless you'll be willing to adopt, which is not a bad option considering the circumstances."

"I would like to shelter the baby in my womb and feel that is really mine."

"Well, then I think you need to find a partner to dance the tango."

"There is my quandary. I will not have casual sex just to be impregnated. I am left with only one alternative and that is to go to an infertility clinic and get a sperm donor."

I met Dr. Peter Amirian, a middle age, cheerful, vivacious obstetrician with whom I discussed the vertiginous roads to achieve success in my new, daring venture. He reassured me that I was not alone in seeking to conceive using a donor. There were many instances of couples where the male was infertile or lesbian couples or like in my case, single women. The process was simple and uncomplicated. At his clinic, it was allowed to choose the sperm donor, who although anonymous could be selected by me taking into consideration personality traits, race, looks, abilities and background, among many other factors. The donor was always subjected to a rigorous physical screening and laboratory tests to validate his apparent good health. The cost of artificial insemination was high, but worth it. I requested after my procedure to destroy the rest of the sperm to avoid the remote possibility that my baby would later meet a sibling without knowing it, and fall in love - an incestuous relationship, a quasi Woody Allen's story. Amirian removed my eggs through a laparoscopic procedure, and after a period of incubation, the embryo was implanted in my uterus.

So that was how Sebastian was born, my beautiful, bubbly, energetic son, the love of my life.

My name is Anthony Stevens. I was born and raised in Wilmington, Delaware. My father was the sole owner of Saint Croix, a successful medical device corporation. His factory employed 50 people, half of which were engineers or specialized technicians. During the years of opulence, my five older sisters and I had an enviable life. We completed our education in England and France. We are a sophisticated bunch of people. We all love the arts, some of us play musical instruments and we all got a college education. I decided at an early age to become a doctor and attended pre-med at Columbia University. For a while it appeared that my road to become a pediatrician was easy and well determined. The only thing I had to do was study and excel. No other worries; I did not have to struggle to pay my tuition.

I did not know, because my dad kept it to himself, that Saint Croix was being sued for having produced one defective implantable cardioverter-defibrillator which caused injury and few deaths. One day, reading the NYT, I became aware that Saint Croix was sued and a jury awarded 60 million dollars to the plaintiffs. I rushed home to find my dad devastated. It was not difficult to image the confluence of things that went wrong. Although my father was not involved in the design of these devices, he felt confident that they were functioning properly, they had been tested in the laboratory and in two clinical trials; their utilization was approved by the Food and Drug Administration. The fact that people died as a consequence of the device was more than my dad could take. Saint Croix went bankrupt, being unable to pay the litigants. The 50 employees at Saint Croix lost their jobs and this aggravated my father's feelings of guilt. He never recovered and died two years later from a heart attack, clearly brought by the ill-fated circumstances.

The Stevens became destitute, yet their inner selves remained intact, their determination to succeed unbroken. We were taught well and knew that our upbringing was going to be enough to pull us back to the path and place where we wanted to be.

I got a college loan, and during my free time I worked in many different jobs. I was a waiter on weekends at Mario's, at times an usher at the Majestic, and did other things to pay for my subsistence.

It was strenuous to work and study, but then I formed a duo of entertainers for children with my friend Vivian, a Biology student at CU. I knew how to perform rather sophisticated magic tricks; she played the guitar and we both sang. It was a high energy performance, full of comedy, laughter and joy. We were paid well and that carried us to the end of our studies.

After finishing Medical School, I applied and was accepted to Children's Hospital in Los Angeles for my residency program. Those three years were stimulating and reinforced my vocation. After graduation I was considering going into pediatric surgery, but my time at Children's convinced me to practice general Pediatrics. I wanted to care for kids face to face.

During the first two years of my residency, I did not have time to enjoy much the allure of Los Angeles; training was brutal; I was working at least 60 hours a week.

I had an intimate relationship with Jessica, also a medical resident at Children's. Our liaison was, looking backward, one of, should I say, convenience with no solid bond. We had good rapport, great sex and enjoyed doing many things together; yet we knew that we were not in love. A year before the end of my training I started looking for a place to practice. There were many decisions to make: I could go into solo practice in New York, an almost insurmountable task, or join a group. I was interviewed by three offices and finally settled with Longhorn Pediatric Associates, a group of eight doctors working near Presbyterian Hospital. I was offered a decent salary and a five year track to become a full partner.

After I became a full-fledged pediatrician I rented an apartment on Brookside Drive in the Village. Three of my sisters came to New York and took over the decorating of my new place. The before and after was remarkable; the place looked like one of those from the pages of the Architectural Digest.

After six months my practice became very busy. I enjoyed my work, New York and my new relationships. Life was good and the sadness of the memories from my father, which had been with me for many years after he died, started to dissipate. I could be happy again.

My mother remarried, two of my sisters got a medical degree and they and the others formed their own families. The only setback was that my family was scattered all over the country. One sister stayed in Wilmington, two moved to San Francisco and the two doctors to Boston, where they opened their own practice, Stevens and Stevens- An Internal Medicine Group.

Gaby was happy again. Sebastian had made her life meaningful. He was an incredible boy, cheerful and jolly, in constant motion, always getting what he wanted, obstinate and tenacious. Gaby was a good mother with an inflexible routine. Sebastian would eat only organic foods; no microwave at home; no television allowed, at least for now; the iPad only for selective games (that he managed like a computer wizard) and every day before bedtime a 20 minute bath. She hired a nanny, Monica, after interviewing and checking into the background of 12 applicants. Monica was a middle age divorcee, Puerto Rican woman. She had two daughters that she raised as a single mother. The girls, Christina and Marissa, attended New York City College and after their graduation they got well paying jobs. Monica adored Sebastian as the son she always wanted to have.

Gaby was given tenure at NYU and was writing a book integrating all of Shakespeare's plays into three, one about tragedies, another about satires and the third about comedies. It was a gargantuan job that took her about four hours a day between compiling, analyzing materials and writing. She was pleased with her life, nothing was missing. Weekends she spent with Sebastian, taking him to music classes, swimming lessons and other joyful activities. She had an active social life, more than she could take. Raul and his friends, who were accomplished artists, became their most trusted group of people to hang around. She saw Rebecca and Spencer, who by then had married and had one child, at least twice a month. The dean of Art School at NYU became a good friend.

 Gaby and Monica would take Sebastian to Dr. Longhorn for his regular checkups. When Longhorn announced that he was retiring, he recommended Dr. Stevens, a bright young doctor, to replace him. She met him for the first time when Sebastian was three years old. He had a way with kids; before putting the tongue depressor in his mouth he would 'magically' make it disappear and that was it. Sebastian would open his mouth because the doctor had to find it; it was somewhere! Even vaccinations became practically painless, a grimace, a frown, no tears. The second time she brought Sebastian for a visit, Gaby had an extended conversation with the new doctor about her life, the death of 'Stone' and the need she felt to have a baby by whatever means. Anthony listened quietly and was somewhat in awe of Gaby. She was beautiful, smart and sensitive.

 After that visit, Monica, who had an extra sense for things, casually asked Gaby what she thought about the looks and demeanor of the new doctor. Gaby admitted that he was handsome and had good bedside manners. "Bedside manners?" Monica, whose command of English was not that good, misinterpreted what bed manners meant and after Gaby explained, they laughed without pause.

One day Gaby, Raul, Rebecca and Spencer went to see Red at The Majestic. After the show, as they were strolling to the street they bumped into Anthony. He was with Vivian, who was visiting from Oregon. They introduced themselves, made casual conversation about the show and started walking in the same direction. By happenstance they all had reservations for dinner at Mario's. Rebecca, who had a third eye for matters of life, asked Anthony and Vivian to share their table. Gaby assumed that Vivian was Steven's girlfriend and he believed that Raul was Gaby's boyfriend.

They had an enjoyable long evening. They first talked about the play; Raul remarked that he found the plot not as good, as Rothko was not represented as he really was. After two bottles of wine the conversation turned more informal; by the end they talked about things that nobody cares about. After a while it was clear that Raul was not Gaby's romantic liaison and Anthony subtly let everybody know that Vivian was just a good friend. He told the story of their working relationship as children entertainers. Raul asked Anthony to do a magic trick for them, he patted him on his chest and then his own and said that he would try, at which time he produced a wallet that belonged to Raul. They were all mesmerized; by the end of the evening they exchanged cell phone numbers and promised to visit again.

When they were walking Gaby home, Raul, Rebecca and Spencer had a subversive look in their face; they did not utter a word but all knew what the others were thinking.

Anthony –"call me Tony"- called Gaby the following week and invited her to have dinner at a new restaurant that had excellent reviews in The New York Times. Although it was hard to make reservations, the chef's little daughter was a patient of his and that assured them a good table. This was how the relationship started. They discovered each other little by little; they began a romantic relationship after several encounters. Anthony understood that he should wait for Gaby to be ready and Gaby realized that Tony was being patient, careful and gentle.

One night after dinner at his place, while they were talking about things of no importance, Gaby embraced and kissed him and felt what she could not feel for years. She was falling in love, Anthony was falling in love; they were in love.

They started sharing days and nights, winter and summer vacations, sunny and rainy times. Their relationship became special for them and for everybody else. Anthony's sisters were very protective of him and did not accept Gaby right away, until they got to know her.

Rebecca was delighted with their relationship and Raul felt that Gaby and Tony had brought Gabby back to life and wherever he was, he was sharing her happiness. During the wedding Sebastian was the joy of the festivity. They settled in a new larger apartment in Manhattan. Time passed and one night Gaby was telling Tony how she went about getting the artificial insemination, described Dr. Amirian as a likable guy with a big ego, and they both laughed when Gaby told that at one time she was considering having casual sex, just to become pregnant, with a handsome stranger that made a pass at her in an Apple Store.

That night Tony could not sleep, he broke out in a fine sweat and tossed around until the next morning.

A week later on a Saturday morning over breakfast:

"Gaby, I am Sebastian's father."

"Of course you are. I cannot think of anybody being so loving, so careful, so nice to Sebastian as you are."

"Gaby, I am his father."

> "Tony, what are you telling me - do you want to adopt him? You want him to be a Stevens; I have to think about it. I appreciate your concern about us. I love you and Sebastian loves you - is this not enough?"

"Have you seen how people always say how he looks like me?"

Yes, that is so common; people always need to make a comment, sometimes he looks like you, sometimes he looks like me, and sometimes he looks like my uncle Eddie..."

"Please, sit. When you told me about Dr. Amirian it brought back to me something that I forgot until now. I told you that when I was in medical school I made money to pay my expenses by doing multiple things. At one time I needed five hundred dollars and I went to Amirian's Clinic to donate my sperm. The night you told me your story I could not sleep until my subconscious brought back my going to the fertility clinic. A week ago I took few strands of hair from Sebastian's hair brush and sent my own cheek smear for a DNA test. They matched. Gaby, I am the father of your child!"

This is a story of love and coincidences.

Aging Gracefully: A contradiction

My name is Lucia D'Lamermour, unrelated to Lucia di Lammermoor or named to honor her, since my ancestors did not know anything about opera.

Like the other Lucia, I had plenty of angst and drama and also happiness during my life.

I have been cursed by my beauty. Only I know how much I tried not to embellish my image. I never used makeup, added ornaments to my body or made fancy with my actions. And yet my lovers found me irresistible because of my naivety, my unpretentiousness and simple manners. I evaded compliments and discerned lust from affection, devotion from obsequiousness. I never married; I had an unexplainable fear to tie myself to any man, no matter how attractive, rich or generous. Even those who took me to the peak of sexual excitement and made my body shake with indescribable pleasure could not engage me to link my life with theirs; I was always longing for a better lover. I caused pain and sorrow to many of them. I was inconsolable when my rejection caused Arturo to kill himself. But that is another story.

Their adoration made me feel more beautiful than I probably was; their devotion fueled me with vigor, their worship enhanced my spiritual strength. I felt whole, nothing was missing from my life and I was happy and possessed what every person aspires: spiritual calm, unmitigated intelligence and wealth.

Don't think that because of my innate attributes I was a quiet, passive, dependent person that needed others to sustain my existence; on the contrary, I was engaged in many activities.

I worked full time in my brother Enrico's company in Silicon Valley. Because of my skills, I was made a minority owner. My task was to improve the performance of the *Luela* computer that he developed in the early eighties. I was able to convince the engineers in the factory to use a sixteen-bit microprocessor that I developed at a rather low cost, which pushed the function of the *Luela* to an incredible performance. After that I was in charge of graphical interfaces and other tasks that made me an invaluable member of the staff.

I made most of my money during the early years of the Internet by registering multiple domain names that I anticipated were going to be of value. It was such a simple venture that I am still perplexed that at the beginning I was one of the very few that came up with the idea.

I had fame and money, which I used to indulge myself in adventures of the mind.

As years went by, my body started showing the passage of time, a situation that I could not bear. For the first time, I felt that I could not be in command. My existence was being altered by biological reasons, which I understood, but could not accept. The degradation of my skin, hair, joints and muscles became a preoccupation that made me gloomy and melancholy.

Suddenly my self-assuredness, self-esteem and the sensation that I was on top of the word started to fade.

I became concerned about the progression of the slow but definite deterioration of my body. At the beginning it was simple: a little makeup would cover my imperfections. Then these shortcomings became more difficult to hide. For a while they were perceptible and tolerable; then less subtle, less understated, more visible and more annoying. I am vain but not to the point that I don't understand the moral and emotional implications of vanity. I knew that I had to alleviate my anguish, which progressed at the same time that my decline hastened. I was slowly descending into a protracted state of fear and sorrow.

Cosmetic surgery was out of the question. It was a temporary relief leading to deformity and converting a person into a permanent caricature.

For a while, I occupied myself with young lovers, who gave me the illusion that I was less old and still attractive and desired. Yet, as all other illusions, they were a chimera from which I got nothing.

I refused to surrender and was not to allow nature to destroy me; at least I was going to put a fight and delay for many years what appeared unavoidable. Being studious, I explored ways to prevent the laxity of my skin, the sagging of my cheeks, the lines under my eyes, the wrinkles in my forehead, the thinning of my lips, the accumulation of fat in my flanks. I improved my eating habits, ate foods rich in antioxidants, little fat and good proteins. I exercised strenuously for three hours a day with the help of a renowned trainer.

Nothing changed.

I came to the conclusion that I had to increase, not stretch, the volume of my face and the only way was to stimulate the production of collagen under my skin. This concept was appealing to many scientists but nobody had achieved that goal. There were hundreds of creams, ultrasonic devices, vibrating apparatuses and a myriad of gadgets that promised to replace the elasticity of the skin. They were all shams.

Finally, I decided to become directly involved in the research and development of a substance to restore the naturally occurring proteins of the connective tissue of the skin, which represents 80% of the skin's dry mass. Botox and soft tissue augmentation by different chemicals were out of the question because they provided short-lasting alleviation and according to my investigations were only 45% effective.

After collecting all available bibliography about the subject I teamed up with Dr. Edgar Ravenswood, who was working with hyaluronic acid. He was a gentle, middle aged, handsome physician, graduated from Harvard, who was eagerly looking to reverse the slow decline of the skin by different methods. He interviewed me for about three hours. He was perplexed at how much I knew so about biology, chemistry, physics and pathophysiology and realized that I had an intelligence quotient much higher than the rest of the population.

We became lovers, which didn't distract us from our main purpose.

We worked hard for one year and enjoyed the excitement of making constant discoveries.

We modified the active component of hyaluronic acid, which became 2-alpha- nonsulfated glycosaminoglycan anionic 3- dextrose-4 lactose acid, tested for safety on animals and reached the conclusion that we had discovered the drug that would bring back their youth to millions of people.

I remember the exhilaration we had when we were ready to inject my face with biotratonic acid, as we called the compound. We did not ask permission to use the drug from the Food and Drug Administration, because we considered that it was an unnecessary, bureaucratic, tenuous government institution; nor did we initiate clinical trials, being certain of its safety and effectiveness. I was to become the first person to test its application.

I remember that day well. The weather was majestic, the skies were clear - an anticipation of better times to come for Edgar and me.

The results were truly astonishing, a dreamlike state of affairs. My cheeks were bony, covered by a perfect skin, as in time past; my creases disappeared; I was young again.

Walking around the casket, nobody failed to repeat and repeat how young I looked; my babyish features were surprising and admired. I received as many compliments as when I was alive and younger.

But don't get carried away with biotratonic acid, as in my case it not only made the wrinkles of the skin disappear, but also the ones from the brain. When the compound reached my forebrain and my midbrain, all their creases disappeared. Comprehension, intellect, sensorial functions and motor abilities were gone in a minute. Don't blame biotratonic for the outcome, because it did what it was supposed to do.

My poor Edgar felt culpable for my demise and killed himself to be reunited with me in the place where looks don't count.

An Ordinary Man

I am a chubby 51 year man with a moderately protuberant belly. My height is 5.5 and my weight 189 pounds. My eyes are brown with almost no eyelashes; over the last 5 years I have been balding. I own two suits, four pair of pants and eight shirts.

When I enter a room nobody notices. Not that I care; in fact, I feel better if left alone.

So now you know: I am not good looking, not charismatic and have kind of a reclusive personality; we can say that I am like millions or billions of other individuals, who do not possess the grace of so many others, like the ones you see in movies and magazines. To be honest, I don't care and have no angst from being who I am. I have limited aspirations in life. I am usually content. My only worries are related to my immediate family.

I am Catholic, as were all my ancestors. I go to church every Sunday, although I am not well versed in the doctrine of our Church. I don't worry about my salvation; I go there to pray for the wellbeing of my wife and my daughter; and after I read an article in Time magazine, for the hungry of this world. Going to church is as much tradition as a distraction; I admire so many things there! The vitrauxs surrounding the altar are of exceptional beauty, the mosaic of different colors and shapes allows the light from the outside to penetrate and gives the figure of Jesus a glow and an aura of purity that I have not seen in any other houses of God. The choir enhances the solemnity of the place with their strident and clear voices that emanate as music from heaven. On top of all these enthrallments, Father Trenton always delivers beautiful sermons. More than the combination of words, what makes him so eloquent is the connotation attached to them. I understood the New Testament for the first time after I listened to this good man. Many things started making sense. Poverty, hunger, rage, wars and many other happenings of life stopped being an abstraction and became real. I started reading the Bible with the purpose of understanding good and evil. I did all of this juggling quietly and kept my thoughts to myself.

My immediate universe is populated by my wife of 21 years, Elaine my daughter Clara, who is 17; my sister and brother-in-law, Jack and Jane; my 12 coworkers and a neighbor across the street, Peter, who has been a widower for eight years. My wife is a teacher at Saint John's Elementary School. She is more outgoing than I am, but like me, she doesn't complain much about the ups and downs of life. She devotes much of her time to preparing her classes and is active in counseling students. I have seen her crying many times after listening to the personal dramas of some of her pupils.

Clara is finishing high school. She is a B student. She has two best friends with whom she hangs around almost every day. As far as I know she doesn't have any boyfriends. Elaine worries a little bit about this, but I think she will worry more the day Clara meets somebody.

What I just told you is in a few words the story of my life; it may not be an exciting one, but I am content.

Life flows almost as if predicted. Mondays to Fridays I work in the office until 5, home before 6, supper at 7, in bed before 11. Breakfast is always eggs with bacon, one toasted piece of rye bread spread with margarine, orange juice from a bottle and black coffee. During the summer and spring we go to the Municipal Rowing Center for recreation on Saturdays, weather permitting. During the winter we go bowling. We visit Elaine's parents, who have been living in a retirement community for the last four years, once a month. They are happy there, have made many friends. They are well attended, there is a van that takes them for doctor's visit when needed, they play Bingo twice a week and those that can still use their legs dance in their Recreation room every Thursday after dinner. They live an exciting life, one that I aspire to have once I retire. I imagine myself winning many of the Bingo contests - how thrilling!

My parents died when I was 25 years old. They were decent people. Dad worked as a foreman for an Israeli contractor for more than 20 years. He learned Hebrew from listening to his boss and his wife, who worked in the firm as an interior designer. My father enjoyed his job and earned a very decent salary. My parents died in a freaky car accident when they were in their fifties.

I inherited the house where we now live.

Our social life entails going out with Jack and Jane to Denis's, a family restaurant, about four times a year, to birthday parties and occasional celebrations from some of our few acquaintances.

I don't have many friends. This is not a dire predicament for me since I don't like to share my infrequent angst or concerns with anybody, even with my wife. Besides, I don't like to make casual talk, something that I see happens frequently at parties and gatherings. One may say that I am a reserved person. Some people believe that I am shy, distant and unfriendly; so be it.

I like watching basketball and football on TV. I don't like to go to movie theaters because it is not uncommon to catch the flu or other viral conditions. The last time we went to the Royal we saw *The Lion King*, which I enjoyed immensely.

Elaine and I make love about once every four weeks when I feel an urge (which I don't know where is coming from). She would never initiate a sexual advance, which is fine with me. The act is short, five minutes at the most, but pleasurable, at least for me. We never talk about making love, it just happens when it happens, although I always ask her for permission.

I am aware that my life is different from most of the people and I don't care. There are millions of things that I don't comprehend, empathize, identify or simply being concerned with. I always vote Republican; they appear to be more patriotic, always ready to defend us, but I like them mainly because they are more in tune with God's teachings. I am appalled by the recent episodes of gun violence. I am in favor of the second amendment because it is in the Constitution, which in my view should be an irrefutable document. I am not sure if background checking before you buy an ammunition is OK or not; perhaps it is a good idea because there are many crazy people out there.

I don't read too much, although I enjoy novels by John Grisham. I may read one or two books a year.

I have been working in an accounting office of a law firm in Sacramento for the last 25 years. I do my job exceptionally well; I am very appreciated by my three bosses. My co-workers sometimes make fun of me behind my back, probably because

I don't talk too much or perhaps because of the way I look. I don't care; in the end I know that I command respect.

Sacramento is a nice city, but in my view is changing for the worse. Over the last ten years it has become noisier and is not as clean as it used to be.

Once, I went to the funeral of my boss James Dixon who had an unexpected heart attack at age 62. Mr. Dixon was a nice guy, jovial and energetic. He treated all the employees with respect; I know he did not like one of his associates, Molly Kruger, the daughter of the founder of the law firm, because she was made a partner, not by merit but for being her father next of kin. I think we call this nepotism, a word with a strong negative connotation.

During the service for Mr. Dixon several people gave a speech commemorating his life and trajectory. I was surprised that somebody I saw every day had accomplished so much. I thought that an exhilarating, electrifying life was the terrain of celebrities and yet there was poor Mr. Dixon having lived a life that I suspect none of the rest of us could ever live. He climbed mountains, played golf with the Attorney General of California, parachuted from planes and gave a lot of money to charities; a wing in the Sacramento Medical Center was named The Dixon Maternity Center after a generous donation. His three children are all Ivy

League graduates. I always knew that there are a group of people that live in a space where I and my family don't have access. They dress and eat differently from us; they never cook their own food; they drive foreign cars and do things in their private lives that are alien to me. Funny, in spite of all his accomplishments, he ended up dying like everybody else. I don't say this with envy; I am repeating what I once read in the *Reader's Digest.*

Listening to his eulogy I imagine what people would say during my memorial service. What could they say about an ordinary man?

When I was young I wanted to become involved in politics. That was the time when I was curious about the events of the world. I got all my information from the Sacramento Bee and realized that nobody in the office or my church was interested in discussing things related to government or global affairs. In 1980 Reagan was contending the presidency from Jimmy Carter. Those were exciting times for me and yet nobody in my circle of acquaintances talked about the election. I noticed a strange disconnect from the ferment and thrill from the media and the people in the streets. Television programs showed vociferous rallies in favor of their candidates, but in my immediate world it looked as this was not happening. As time passed I became disenchanted with politics because the government was doing exactly the opposite of what I thought was right for the people. These earlier experiences made me more reclusive.

I am telling my story because of something that happened recently that I still do not understand.

I was sitting in a sidewalk savoring a cup of coffee in the Starbuck's located adjacent to the Filmore train station. I was waiting for a client, who was arriving from Fresno for a business meeting, to discuss the development of a casino in Reno with my bosses, who asked me to pick him at the station and then drive him to the office. As I was gazing around I noticed two young good-looking couples having fun, chatting and laughing. There was also a vivacious child, about four years old, eating an ice cream, probably the daughter of one of the couples. She was cute, had blonde hair and reminded me of Clara as a kid. The day was splendid, sunny and dry. I think people were jubilant because of the nice weather. After that I don't remember anything else.

So I am going to let Father Trenton tell the rest of the story:

Let us thank God for the opportunity we are given to honor a family man, a friend, a hero, a brave man who Jesus put in this Earth with a purpose. You may want to understand why the Lord has taken Jonathan's life so early, at the peak of his life.

His wife and daughter had an unconditional love for this person who filled their life with joy and happiness. He was appreciated by friends and co-workers. So why him? Why did our kind, noble Jonathan die in such tragic circumstances?

We may be consoled to know that death is not the end but the beginning of our communion with the Trinity, where we will achieve definitive peace and happiness. Our friend has died in God's grace and by his deeds in this earth; he has assured his Eternal salvation.

Let's lift up our spirits, because for Jonathan this is not the end but the beginning of a better life.

The circumstances of his passing were those of a true hero.

People were at the Filmore station waiting for a train to arrive. Some were pacing the platform; others were reading the morning newspaper. Jonathan was waiting for a client in a coffee place adjacent to the station. Annie, a beautiful, curious, perky girl, walked toward the rails, bypassing the lowered crossing gates. The conductor of the train saw her, applied the brakes as hard as he could and activated the siren. Jonathan turned around and without hesitation, jumped toward Annie, pushed her away from the incoming wagon and suffered the thump. Jonathan died; Annie was saved.

And yet he was saved, too. Our Lord Jesus Christ has a special place for those who have an instinctive behavior toward goodness. He did not measure the risk of what he was about to do. His only impulse was to save the life of the child. He did not require any special skills to do what he did. It came from his heart; fear did not override his actions. Annie's life was to be saved; Jonathan did what he knew he had to do.

You see, dear parishioners: Jonathan was not an ordinary man.

Spinocrates Junior the III (1940-1999)

Like other perishables, marriage should come with an expiration date.

Spinocrates Senior the II (1922- 1970)

Hoarding is not a vice. Is a vice, vice, vice, vice, vice, vice, vice, vice, vice, vice, vice, vice, vice, vice, vice….

Back to School

In 1976 I was offered a position as a research fellow at Yale University. I eagerly, and with my wife's blessings, accepted it. It was an enviable academic position in one of the most prestigious institutions of the United States; as a secondary gain I was going to get away and avoid political persecution in Argentina, my beloved country of origin, the one that gave me the opportunity to get a medical degree tuition-free. In Argentina education was accessible to everybody. Today we call it socialism, but at that time there was no discussion, even among opposite political parties, that people deserved an education, a conviction shared by the right and the left. There was one private University, sponsored by the Catholic Church, and even there the tuition was negligible. That was the reason that a country of 40 million people produced so many brilliant academicians and scientists, including several Nobel Prizes. I always felt indebted to Buenos Aires University for providing me with the opportunity to excel in my professional endeavors.

When the offer came I had mixed feelings; I was convinced that for the sake of my career the chance to work in the States was the right thing to do, but I also felt that I was abandoning a sinking ship, leaving behind friends and family, and I was somewhat disloyal, tearing the blanket that until then had protected me and gave me the opportunity to be who I am today.

Once I accepted, it became my mission: I was going to apply all my strength to excel in my new position.

I erased all doubts and with firm determination went for the adventure of my life, one that would change everything for me: Juan Carlos Mendez, PhD; Dr. Maria Mendez, my wife, a renowned sociologist, and my kids.

My twins, Elena and Marcelo, who were nine years old, were not happy to leave their friends and cousins behind, but went along with our decision without a full comprehension of the circumstances that pushed us to move to a new country.

My parents cried. It was the first time I saw my mother shedding tears, which I didn't know if they were coming from nostalgia or pride. My father also cried, but that didn't concern me much; he was a guy that would sob for a whole lot of things: a sentimental movie, a tragedy reported in the newspaper, seeing a dog limping, not to mention his kids getting married and other transcendental things. Interestingly enough the only time I expected a fountain of tears was when his older brother died, but he kept silent and quiet, without a whimper; God only knows what his emotions were at that moment. Perhaps he became solemn to show that now that he became the senior member of the family, he could control himself or perhaps he had some subconscious resentment toward his sibling that we were never aware of.

The trip to New York was memorable. Marcelo cried during the entire trip; perhaps he inherited the trait from his grandfather. Elena and Maria were quiet. I was bubbly talking all the time with the stewardess and some of my fellow passengers. Maria, who knows a lot about behavior, asked me to calm down; I was having a manic episode from the volatile mix of joy and apprehension.

When we arrived my English was rudimentary, but I was able to get by with I had learned for three years in high school; my wife Maria was the 'official translator', having learned the language in a British Academy in Buenos Aires, and the twins had not a grain of understanding of either spoken or written English. Yet it was surprising how they could communicate non-verbally or gutturally with their new friends from the first day of our arrival.

I observed them playing for hours with their new friends and talking to each other in Spanglish, the dialect of beginners. But the neurons in their brain were in the right place, and functioning at perfect speed. The bridges between them were intact, so in a few months, not years, they were both speaking English like natives. I tried to make English the first language at home, but as soon as I talked they immediately switched to Spanish, something they didn't do with their mother. I didn't say anything about this but I could not help feeling inferior when it came to communication; anyway, Spanish became the first language and English the second in our household

At Yale, foreign graduates were encouraged not to use their native language for the first year, watch only English speaking television and read only in the English language. It was mandatory to listen to audio tapes to improve our language and grammar skills at the Library, two hours a day, five days a week. The results were astonishing. I acquired optimal command of the language with an extensive vocabulary and exceptional syntaxes. After one year Elena and Marcelo spoke perfect English, undistinguishable from other kids, and Maria became highly skilled in the new vernacular. After two years I was able to use slang (*cold fish, goofed up, honcho* and others), something that my wife could not master, but she got a grasp of some idioms (*a dime a dozen, Elvis has left the building, an axe to grind*, and others). I could understand the words in isolation but it took me a long time to figure out the meaning of *kicked the bucket, to make ends meet, to pay through the nose.*

In spite of this progress something was missing - or not? I had an accent, a heavy one.

People responded to my speech in different ways. Their reaction made me box them in five groups.

The Puritans: Those who would never ask me about my origins. I have known many like them; they are the ones that are always polite, will never utter their feelings in public, they are never blue or red, always white; I felt uncomfortable around them because I never knew what their feelings were.

The *Liberal*s: Those that as soon as they heard my accent would ask me 'where are you from?' I was more at home with them, because they were never reticent to speak their mind. If you say Good Morning and it was raining outside they would respond 'what's good about it'. When the door of the elevator opened they would command all passengers with a 'ladies first.' As years passed this was the group with whom I had a sense of belonging, and some of them became my acquaintances.

The Romantics: Their query always started with 'what a lovely accent you have; where are you from?' I loved them, although at times I felt uncomfortable because I could not read them well. Did they really mean that my accent was lovely? Anyway, I accepted their compliment as a fact and responded with a smile.

The Realists: The ones that after hearing my accent would ask, 'How long have you been in this country?' delivering a message of disapproval in a tangential way. I hated these bastards; their comments had a tinge of racism and condescendence.

Finally, The Smart Asses: They always wanted to guess where I was from: French? Israeli? Yugoslavian? My answer was always the same: I am from Iowa, at which time they cracked up and stopped asking.

Years passed and little by little, right or wrong, I believed that my accent was a hindrance. I had problems with th. Elena, who has motherly instincts, tried to help me. "Dad, put your tongue behind your upper teeth and say 'month'." No way, I could not do it. V and B for me were the same: a boy was a boy and vertical was bertical. Here I succeeded. "Dad, for a V you should bite your lower lip"; this is how bertical recovered and became one more time vertical, and Victor, Advantage, Vortex and hundreds of other words recovered from my vocal assassination.

One evening I was trying to buy tickets to fly to Florida over the phone. I called **American Airlines**, was connected to their automated services and was prompted, (by the way, with a voice that I also recognized when calling the Gas Company, a Department store and many others): **Which is your departure city?** I answered Los Angeles, then: **Which is your arrival city?** Fort Lauderdale, I replied. What date? October twenty-first. Diligently the Interactive Voice Response, needing confirmation, said: **You want to travel**

from Los Angeles to Asuncion, Paraguay, on September first, is that right?

Oh boy!, I hate these machine conversations so much; no matter how much you try, you cannot reach a human being, somebody with flesh, bones and a soul.

I hastily hung up, got into a depressive state and decided that it was time to take accent reduction classes. It was back to school.

It was not easy to get the right instructor. A lot of them advertised on the Internet, but who? I dismissed many: some were arrogant, others boring and dull, and most of them just trying to make a buck to complement their income, but not with the empathy I was looking for.

I finally settled with a chap recommended by the Public Relations Department at YU. Makito was an affable Japanese fellow, who himself had a slight accent. He came to the US when he was 12 years old and with the help of an instructor improved his intonation and accent and advanced his conversational skills. I was reluctant to engage a foreigner to help me but decided that if I were to fail in this endeavor, I could always blame the teacher.

Makito came to our training sessions equipped with a book and a plastic straw. He would make me read the passage of a chapter, identify the words I had problems with, correct me and made me repeat them again and again until I got them right. A rose for me was a *rös*, not a *roz*; hair was *jai*r and not *haer*. Makito would make me listen to my new improved inflection by repeating those words into one end of the straw, while the other end was buried into my ear. After six months, either out of compassion or realism, he terminated the instruction, emphasizing that although I was going to take my accent to the grave, from now on people would not have any problems understanding my English.

I really liked him. I embraced him and we wished each other well.

Before saying goodbye he gave me three pieces of advice: one was to speak slowly; second to use difficult words to make my interlocutor feel inferior; and finally, to renounce my self-deprecating humor.

I was happy; people would not ask me to repeat words again and again.

The day came when I happily called my sweet Maria and the twins for the test of my life.

Until then, I had kept secret all about my accent reduction classes. I wanted to surprise them with my newly learned skill.

They did not know why I summoned them, but eagerly saw me in action.

Anxiously I dialed **American Airlines** and the automated service prompted, **Choose one from the following menus....** *Reservations?* I answered yes. **Which is your departure city?** *Los Angeles* **And your arrival city?** *Fort Lauderdale.* **What day?** October twenty-third.

American Airlines: You would like to travel from Los Angeles to Portland, Oregon, on October twentieth, is that right?

"Well," Maria said,"at a least Portland is closer than Asuncion, Paraguay, and you only have to take the plane two days earlier."

OBITUARIES

My name is Gina Petrucelli. My husband, Enrico Salvaterra, died yesterday, July 2, 2013. He was born in Brindisi exactly 26 years ago. He attended Certicento High School, where he barely obtained his Baccalaureate. Only after bribing the Principal of the school was a Diploma granted. We married at the Basilica de San Marcos three years ago. The first two years of our marriage, we lived a life full of joy and happiness. Over the last year he became aloof and inattentive to my emotional and physical needs. He constantly changed jobs, having worked as a carpenter, a book binder and lately a cook's aid in Longorio's Pizzeria. He was not making enough money and in order to pay the rent of our beautiful apartment I was forced to go back to work at Messina's Shoe Store.

Yesterday, I caught him celebrating his birthday, having sex in our home during his noon break with Marina Manitutti, a 21 year old friend of mine. The scene was grotesque; they were performing the act completely naked and in front of a mirror, something that he never offered to do with me.

At that very time he became literally dead for me,forever. I don't want to see or hear from him again. He is as good as a dead fish. He is survived by his mother Carla, who cooks the worst pasta that I ever tried, his sister Maria, who has been dumped five times by potential suitors, and his youngest brother Giovanni who is and always will be a moron. *

Published in Corrieri de la Sera, July 3, 2013.

*Translated from the Italian by Luigi Graziano.

BIRTH ANNOUNCEMENTS

My name is Enrico Salvaterra. I would like to announce that I was born again on July 2, 2013, after being dumped by my wife Gina Petrucelli. I had been married for three long, unbearable years. The first week of my marriage was full of joy and happiness, soon to be replaced by an existence of acrimony, bitterness and bad blood. Gina became demanding and made me change jobs on three different occasions. She wanted a life of leisure and luxury, while I wished to come to a home of tranquility and harmony. I expected Gina to cook pasta the way my mother does, always al dente, with the best sauces in the world. Or be like my sister Maria, who had a flair and knack for men, who are crazy about her.

Today I feel like a new man, free and independent. I will become again the smiley, flamboyant guy that I used to be. I am now liberated from the constraints of the recent past. Thanks to Marina Manitutti for having been the trigger of my rebirth.*

Published in Corrieri de la Sera, July 4, 2013.

*Translated from the Italian by Giovanni Salvaterra (Enrico's brother).

NOTICE FROM THE EDITOR

My name is Euripides Benvenutti. Last week this newspaper inadvertently published two announcements, one in Obituaries and the other in the Birth Section, that did not conform with our Editorial Policy:

(www.CDLS.com/publishingguidelinesformorons)

Therefore, I am forced to remind our readers that Obituaries will in the future accommodate death announcements of persons of any age, sex or sexual orientation who have not been able to breathe or maintain a heartbeat for a minimum of 24 hours. On the other hand, Birth Notices will be reserved for those who have come to life from the womb of a mother within one week of the event.*

Corrieri de la Sera, July 1, 2013

*Translated from the Italian by Charles Friedman, Paul Brooks and Gail Dowd from the New York Times

Deconstructing the Establishment

I am haunted by a dreadful existential question. Are my friends and I Antiestablishment, as we call ourselves?

We believe we are; our political and social views differ from most of the people.

To us it is a given that the Kennedy assassination was part of a conspiracy; the Church is an anachronistic, self-serving institution, where corruption is rampant; corporations are greedy and socially irresponsible; they commit crimes which are made legal by the Congress, who are bought by money from lobbyists; the ruling class lacks transparency, and they exert their action under an impenetrable cloud; the wars in Iraq and Afghanistan were a creation of the industrial-military establishment; we believe that the only way to finish the war on drugs is to legalize them; women and minorities continue to be debased and power corrupts, is exploitive and unjust.

On the other hand, the Establishment adheres to an idealistic normative behavior and a conservative lifestyle.

It not easy, in real life, to define what constitutes the ideological core of antiestablishment.

Like most of my friends, I drive an expensive European car, have a fulltime housekeeper, live in a luxurious mansion in the Hollywood Hills and have a fat checking account.

It is precisely my lifestyle, my possessions and my aspirations that may give the impression that in reality I (and my friends) are cynics, and the only way to avoid this epithet is to either keep quiet or renounce to the cherished title of Antiestablishment, keep our opinions to ourselves and/or carry on with our behavior but without a label.

Deep inside we will feel that we are truly anticonventional and we are proud to be to the left of the political spectrum.

I know people like us that are against the established social status and live like we do.

 My beloved Sean Penn embraces all the things I care for and lives the life of a magnate; others like Oliver Stone, my idol; the master of controversy, Noam Chomsky; Paul Moyers and many others that share my craving for peace, social justice and equality work and live inside the system as I do. This has increased my perplexity.

I need to know who I am and where I belong. I can no longer accept doubt.

When uncertainty is a temporary state of mind it leads to creativity, but if persistent, it leads to madness.

Since I know that my dilemma affects millions of people like me, I have devised a contraption that will define who we are.

This is a rather simple test; there are two columns with facts that are inherent to one of the two groups. The reader ascribes himself one or the other and the more prevalent defines the individual.

ESTABLISHMENT	**ANTIESTABLISHMENT**
Mercedes Benz	Prius
The Wall Street Journal	The New York Times
Peoples Magazine	The New Yorker
Beverly Hills	Culver City
Polo Shirts	No brand
Newport	Venice Beach
Rolex	Timex
Safeway Supermarket	Trader Joe's
Disneyland	St. Bart
John Grisham	Naomi Klein
Four Seasons Hotel	Boutique Hotels
Extramarital Affairs	Extramarital Affairs
Charity	Political Contribution
American Airlines	Virgin Airlines
Socks	No socks

Cheating on Taxes	Cheating on Taxes
Sound Sleeper	Insomnia
No Psychotherapy	Psychotherapy 3 times a week
Poor Tipper	Good Tipper
Fifty Shades of Gray	Planet of Slums
George Bush	Fidel Castro
Hamburger and Fries	Sea Bass and Beets
Macy's	Neiman Marcus
Colgate Tooth paste	Tom's
Sex once a week	Sex every day
HMO	PPO
Bank of America	Banque Pictet (Hong Kong)
Pension Plan: 250,000	Pension Plan: 5,000,000
Time magazine	The New Yorker
iPhone 4	iPhone 5
Golf	Tennis
Budweiser	Anchor Steam

Two Sisters and One Brother

Chela

Seventy-three – eight, four, two, four.

There is no answer at the end of the line.

I wanted to hear your voice

One more time.

I know

You are gone -

How many years now?

Forty-six.

It was a cruel cancer

That took you away.

I still can see your smile,

Your brown eyes,

Your blond hair.

You were so young

And I loved you so much.

You left five children.

They are doing well.

I remember your poise,

Your laughter...

Well,

I will call again.

I don't care

That there is no answer at the end of the line.

Elsita

Forty-three – one, one, one, zero.

There is no answer at the end of the line.

I know.

I called anyway.

I miss you so much.

Perhaps,

Who knows?

You may answer one more time.

But you are gone;

Your heart gave up.

The doctors told Mammy

You wouldn't last,

But you fooled them

For fifty years.

When I called you

You were not there.

Perhaps your face flushed

As when we played those games.

Call me again

By my diminutive nickname,

As you did before,

When we were kids.

Tell me about

Your perennial boyfriend

One more time.

I listened before;

I will listen now.

Everybody

Loved you so much -

Your cousins, your siblings, your aunts

Your friends...

Well, you are not there.

I don't care.

I will call you again.

Luisito

Eighty-four – four, two, six, two.

There is no answer at the end of the line.

I wanted to talk

One more time.

I know you are gone.

How old were you?

Fifty-six

Oh my, how young…

A brutal cancer -

Unexpected, uninvited, undesired -

Took you away.

Another of my siblings…

Now I have only one left.

Remember in Padua

What a good time we had

When we told the porter

To let us in

Because we were

Torquato Tasso's great-grandkids?

I was a little bit jealous

Because Mammy

Loved you more,

But I loved you also -

A lot.

I miss you;

Your sleeping late,

Always tardy

To work...

Who cares now?

We cared then.

I even miss

Your ups and downs.

I even miss

When you made me laugh,

When you made me cry.

I lived far away

From you

In miles -

A short distance

In my heart.

Well, you are not there.

I will call again.

Perhaps

We can talk one more time -

Who knows?

You may answer with a smile.

After all,

We are Torquato Tasso's great-grandkids.

Exquisite Synchronicity

Friends are forever, so they say. Tilda was turning 49 on March 12 and my wife Sabrina was going to celebrate her friend's birthday with an extravagant meal, as she has done over the last seven years. Sabrina is an incredible cook, inventive and original.

We have a ritual: she would allow me to see the raw food material that she used and then kick me out of the kitchen while she was cooking and voila! Like magic, a most sumptuous, elegant meal would appear on the table. That day I fulfilled my duties, preparing the cocktails, choosing the wine.

Tilda was an opinionated woman. She was born in Fresno, California. Her parents were both teachers, lived comfortably in a middle class neighborhood and raised Tilda and her sister Marla with restrained love. Marla was an astounding beauty, charismatic and intelligent. She went to Silicon Valley to work as a software engineer and two years later married her boss Brian, who had made a fortune developing an application for the Internet.

Tilda met Jeffrey when she was twenty-four years old. He was a scientist working at Caltech in Pasadena, California.

Tilda worked as a high school teacher for two years, decided that this was not her calling and with a friend opened a paper store where they sold cards, stationary, pens, journals and collectibles.

It took her three years to figure out that this was not what she wanted to do; after being idle for a few years she worked as a manager in a dental office. She found the job unfulfilling and after delivering Preston, her only son, decided to become a mom and a housekeeper.

Jeff was a rigid scientist who worked hard, sometimes 16 hours a day. He loved Caltech and would spend his spare time in their club and the library.

Tilda felt neglected. Jeff would forget their anniversary; if she wore a new hairstyle he would not notice; he would never become aware of a new dress; or perceive that a new dish was prepared to surprise him.

Preston was raised by Tilda; Jeff became an absent father.

Little by little Tilda became sour and started quarreling with Jeff more and more.

As usual, people squabble over little things, nothing important: being late for a dinner date, leaving the heater on when they were not in the house (adding to the electrical bill), forgetting to bring back her dress from the cleaners. At times it was more substantive things like not paying enough attention to their son, never going to see him playing with his soccer team and other things that he considered banalities and Tilda an important action so Preston would not feel that he was raised without a father.

Fights were the way they expressed the frustration over their relationship; she wanted to love and be loved; he wanted a recreational companion who would devote her time to take care of him and calm his sexual urges. He lived in a tower, devoting more time to his brain than to his emotions.

My wife, a social worker, told me that that a therapist, Steve De Shazer, took two variants - stability and satisfaction - and mixed them to create four categories of couples: stable satisfactory, stable unsatisfactory, unstable unsatisfactory and unstable satisfactory. De Shazer recommended therapists to place their clients in one of them before starting treatment to serve as a point of reference.

She decided that Tilda and Jeff had a stable unsatisfactory liaison; after all, for one reason or another, they have been together more than 28 years.

Sabrina, an admirer of intellect and innovation, once told me how much she would like to develop a bottom line, catchy phrase to identify some life situation like De Shazer did.

That night we had a lovely dinner. Everything was homemade, from the appetizers to the dessert. We talked, laughed and ate. Then it was time for Tilda to blow the candles and open her birthday card. The card was meant to be funny but as it usually happens it was not, but she smiled anyway. The cake was crowned by one candle representing the other forty-eight.

As she was about to go ahead with the ritual of blowing the candle she was reminded that she had to make one wish. "A real one, which has to come from your desires, needs or aspirations; think about your goals and aims. Do it intensely with inner, indomitable force so it may become a reality," I said.

She closed her eyes. At that very time we felt that the air turned cold; there was an inaudible vibration in the atmosphere; we all remained silent. A few seconds later she blew the candle; at the same time Jeff dropped his chin to his chest, had a cardiac arrest and died.

Days later Sabrina told me that she had named the incident "exquisite synchronicity"; her fame was about to come.

Inspiration

Good Morning. Welcome to the Department of Creative Writing of the University of Miami.

For a change, it is a beautiful, warm, shiny day. Yesterday's storm is gone; it looks like good weather is here to stay.

Today, we are going to discuss the methods that authors use to write fiction stories.

There is not one single technique, but rather as many as there are writers, or aspiring writers.

For didactic purposes we will discuss two, which are at the end of a wide spectrum.

One is the one that an author uses following a rigid protocol. Everything starts with an idea which becomes the foundation of a story; this is followed by writing the treatment. This is generally used to write the script for a movie but by extension we can understand the process as useful to write fiction stories, biographies, non-fiction or any type of narrative prose. This is followed by a depiction of all the characters; they get a name, a personality, a physical appearance and a role. Once this is achieved the author scribbles hundreds of notes; this helps to write and rewrite a plot. Once the concept of - let's say - a play is outlined, the components are shuffled, the dialogues created and the essence of the subject is written in a way that will show the genius and the gifts of the writer. In essence, the writing of the tale starts with the expansion of the core of the story.

Fifty Shades of Grey had a simple premise: stories written around the love affair of a student and a business magnate. What made this book so popular was the description of sexual practices of dominance and submission. Other situations explained in the book are otherwise non-essential; only the excuse to introduce sex as the main narrative.

When using this technique writing flows easily, without interruption. It is difficult to believe that when using this method, an author may develop writer's block, or the need to call a muse for inspiration. Anyway, any respectable writer knows that in real life there is no Terpsichore.

For better understanding, this method is in some way similar to that one uses to cook: first comes the decision of what you want to eat, then get all the different ingredients that go into preparing the meal, followed by the combination of the components, add spices, and choose the cooking temperature until the tidbit crystallizes.

The other type of writer - the one we are going to discuss in length today - uses a method which provides him/her a continuous sense of exhilaration. They write without a preconceived script; rather, they link each occurrence as they evolve.

I call this method Progressive Concatenation.

I will guide you through the process with an example, which is also your assignment for the next few weeks:

The author, let's call her Sheila, writes the word *Marie*. This is a French name and the one that initiates plot. Then she writes: *Marie goes to the Boulangerie to fetch a baguette.* The reader is guessing, right or wrong, that Marie is in France. Sheila now describes the streets and the shops, to provide a picture of the habitat. *Marie crosses Rue Bonaparte in the 6th Arrondisement to go back home.* So yes, she is in Paris. The author is building positive expectations by allowing us to identify right away with Marie; who wouldn't like to be in Paris, the romantic city of the world? Let's continue: *She is at the sidewalk when a young man in rudimentary French asks her if she speaks English. "Mais oui, how can I help you?" "I need to take a train to Lyon. Would you know how I can get there" "Bien sure, the Station is half a block from here; take the southbound train. It will deposit you*

160

right in the Gare de Lyon." The author does not know exactly where the story is going; she has the same expectations as the reader. Is Marie young, pretty, an intellectual? Who is this young English-speaking chap?

The protagonists have a conversation. Sheila now depicts the physical attributes of the protagonists and the feelings that they slowly appear to experience after their first encounter.

An intense romance develops between them. Marie is 45 years old and he, Byron, is 25. The age difference of the two lovers becomes the Gordian knot of the story. Here is where the talent of the author may become evident.

Marie is a professor at Le Sorbonne and Byron is planning to spend two years in Europe (this is his first trip to the Continent) to get a master's degree as a museum curator, and in the meantime travel all around Europe where the distances between regions are short.

Sheila describes colorfully the sexual encounters of Marie and Byron - vividly, without any constraints. Sheila decides that she will lure her audience with scenes of love and passion that will make the reader want to read more. Sex sells books. The more explicit and graphic, the better. No inhibitions or vagueness; no unambiguous depictions. This book is a mixture of romance and a mystery story.

When Sheila started writing this work of fiction she did not have any idea where she wanted to go. Not by design, but it looks like she is writing a detective story. The links of the script started with the word Marie; now a plot is being concocted.

Sheila is not sure whether to take an easy road and write an interesting narrative or delve into the psychology of the protagonists and make the novel more profound, a la Flaubert. Since Marie and Byron have a 20 year difference in age, Sheila decides to write about love in the sphere of divergent ages.

Marie realizes that there is more than sex in their relationship and she is truly in love with Byron; she perceives that it is reciprocal. She worries about the future; when she is 65 years old, Byron will be only 45. An old lady with a young man, she thinks. Would it be better to terminate the relationship right now? Or live in the present and forget about miseries that may never come? Would she need to discuss her angst with Byron?

Sheila will compound the storyline with a serious discussion of matters of the heart.

Conan Doyle provided Sherlock Holmes with logical reasoning and forensic knowledge to solve difficult cases. Byron will use his knowledge of the human condition, which he learned from the life of many artists, to resolve the quandaries of his relationship; Marie will use her instincts. She used to have a sixth sense about matters of the heart; will she be able to apply it to the present situation?

They were a happy couple. People never noticed that there was a 20 year difference between them. Marie looks younger and after their relationship she developed a radiant glow that made her feel like a an adolescent.

The next chapters describe their friends and happenings at work in order to lay the foundation for what is about to come. Let's jump now into the core of the book:

Then tragedy struck. Byron arrived late in the night after a twenty day absence. He had gone to London for a workshop about faked art. It was an excellent meeting. This was a hands-on clinic. During the last five days of the meeting, falsified and real Monet, Manets, Bruegels and Tintorettos were brought to be discriminated by the students. He enjoyed the practicum and the camaraderie between teachers and students. He met a young Australian - charming and intellectually challenging student - by the name of Crystal, with whom he developed a special rapport. Byron really liked her; they had dinner together several times and only his devotion to Marie stopped him from fulfilling his fantasies.

When he arrived in Paris and opened the door of Marie's apartment, he saw Marie lying in a pool of blood; she was dead. She had been stabbed in the chest. He was in shock and could not move for several minutes; he looked around and saw no signs of a violent entry. In fact, the door was locked when he arrived. His mind started to spin around. Somebody who had a key killed her. It took him a while to collect himself and put his thoughts together; then he called the police.

Detective Jean Lucien was a gentle middle aged gentleman, who looked more like a salesman than a policeman. While his colleagues were busy taking fingerprints, pictures and sealing areas of the flat, he told Byron that although he was not considered a suspect, he would appreciate if he could stay in Paris and surrender his passport...

Your assignment, my dear students, during this 22-day break, is to write the conclusion of the novel. I would advise to continue with the Progressive Concatenation method since it may give some continuity to the project. You need to connect the links of the story to wrap it up. It will be fun, I promise. Although not an absolute requirement, you may want to consider, since this is a detective story, finding out who killed her. Any other twist to the narrative is acceptable.

Two days later the *Miami Herald* had a headline on their front page with a picture: Sheila Grant, a Literature Professor at MU, was found dead in her apartment, and a subtitle: Found by her boyfriend, who is 20 years younger.

Police told us that they will use the Progressive Concatenation Method for the investigation, which in the past has helped them solve difficult crimes.

Facts and Statistics

I am a statistician graduated from Princeton University in 1981. I have been teaching and doing research on the subject for the last 32 years and I love it. Statistics are so telling!

The definition of Statistics - a compilation and quantitative interpretation of the significance of data - is simple and yet complicated, in that it does not tell the entire concept without further elaboration.

Stating that there are 254 million registered vehicles in the US is a fact, not a statistic; on the other hand, information about ownership of vehicles according to ethnic groups, driver age, number of accidents for each different car and other variables becomes a statistic because it goes beyond one single datum and provides the opportunity to understand the complexities of a subject matter.

I am so immersed in this field that I neglected a social life and dedicated most of my existence to designing experiments to improve the quality of information. When I start a project, I become so absorbed and excited that I cannot stop working until I reach a definitive conclusion.

People say that you can manipulate statistics to reach the conclusions you want to get. This is true to a certain extent, but never when the numbers are coming from me.

The problem is correlation of data. I will give the reader two examples: one gross and one fine instance of problems with interpretation of information. The first one is obvious, the other is not. In 1943 Streptomycin, an antibiotic, was first isolated by Albert Schatz at Rutgers University. Three years later a randomized trial proved that this drug was the first effective treatment in curing pulmonary tuberculosis, a condition that previously had been fatal in large numbers of affected patients. That same year, 1946, people with TB receiving Streptomycin in Buenos Aires were getting cured. At the same time, electric street cars were excluded from circulation in the city. One could then make the assumption that the disappearance of TB was due to the removal of the vehicles; clearly a terrible and absurd misconception.

Another study correlating annual income and age of death showed that poor people have shorter life spans. Although true, in this case there are concurrent and confounding factors; for instance, a high rate of fatal crimes in the purported population makes the association less clear in its significance. Is death due to poverty, crime, malnutrition, sanitation or housing, or some other factor?

Lately, I found it interesting that, better than statistics, certain plain data may illuminate, entertain or make people think about the nature of human beings. I initiated this compilation of information when I became acutely annoyed by the observation of the acute inequality of humans in different parts of the world. It is as if they are two kinds of people inhabiting the planet: the privileged and the unprivileged ones, the masters and their subjects, the landlords and their servants, the exploiters and the exploitees, the politicians, the celebrities, the magnates, the aristocrats on the high end of the see-saw and the peasants, the laborers, the unemployed, the misers on the lower end. There is a kind of indecency in the social structure. When I was young it appeared to me that this inequality was going to become extinct, due mainly to the progress of science and technology. I thought that the road of fair distribution of riches started during the French Revolution and was going to slowly and inexorably reach its zenith. But no, only the dresses have changed; the powerful are still the powerful, the others are the oxen pushing the carts.

I call this simple collection of numbers and records combined with statistical data <u>actuarial social</u>

analysis, opposite to actuarial science, which is used to assess risk in the finance and insurance industries. In healthcare, for instance, it is used to deny services to those who are deemed to be a burden to the balance sheet of the insurance companies.

What you are about to read is factual and indisputable. The meaning is a matter of interpretation; because I am a mathematician I will leave the inference of this information to you.

The following descriptive facts contain information that may not be suitable for sensitive and caring people.

Fact: A Patek-Philippe Perpetual Calendar watch is listed at $82,900.00. Its function encompasses telling hours, minutes, seconds and having a perpetual calendar. At Mateo Jewelers it appears to be a bargain because its retail price is $99,200.00. At World of Watches a comparable Stuhrling Original Men's Aviator Calendar Swiss Quartz sells for $144.67. As accurate and reliable as the Patek-Philippe, it also tells hours, minutes and seconds. And has a calendar!

Statistics: According to the United States Department of Health and Human Services a family of four making $23,050 is in a state of privation and cannot fulfill their basic needs such as food, clothing, and shelter. There are 43.6 million people in the United States living under the poverty line according to the U.S. Census Bureau. To be lifted from poverty a family of four needs to be making more than $23,050.

Bottom Line: At least three and three-quarter destitute families may be lifted from the poverty line by the price of <u>one</u> Patek-Philippe each year.

Fact: Sandy Will, former chairman of Citigroup, sold his penthouse at 15 Central Park West to a Russian billionaire for $88 million.

Statistics: In Indiana the median sales price for a house is $84,000 in a residential area. There are an estimated 22,000 homeless individuals in the great state of Indiana.

Bottom line: The price of the NY condominium can buy 104 houses in Indiana and lodge 912 otherwise homeless people.

Fact: There are one billion malnourished people in the world at a given time.

Statistics: Forty million tons of food is wasted by household and food services each year alone.

Bottom Line: Avoiding this would suffice to satisfy the food needs of every individual in the world. Reducing food waste has additional benefits, like saving money and improving the environment.

Fact: A Hermes Kelly Handbag Etain retails for 17,999.00 USD.

Statistics: The median annual income for a worker in Somalia is 150 USD and the unemployment rate is 50%.

Bottom Line: For the price of one Kelly handbag one could employ 120 people in Somalia for one full year.

I will leave to sociologists, ethicists, theologians, politicians, teachers, clergy, and others, including you, my loyal reader, to analyze, interpret and decode the data that I presented. I only chose four correlations, although there are several thousand significant ones in the Universe; but I felt so gloomy citing the above that I had to stop writing to maintain my sanity.

Finally

Good evening and welcome everyone. This Conference is being broadcast live all over the Planet. My name is Günter Silesia; I am the Secretary of Health for the United Nations.

I am proud to announce that for the first time in the history of the world, we can affirm without any reservations that hunger has disappeared from the Universe.

It has been a gargantuan effort to reach this situation; once we determined that there was more than enough food on this Earth, it was a matter of assuring its proper distribution to each human being, something we achieved by placing all the resources of technology in the right place.

Today, there is not one single individual that will go to bed hungry. Moreover, I can attest that all common edibles contain the nutrients, vitamins, minerals and proteins that have made malnutrition or dietary deficiencies a thing from the past.

Three decades ago we conquered Diseases - with a capital D - which a century ago were prevalent, affecting billions of persons.

We can today proudly assert that hypertension, diabetes, coronary disease, cancer and all other ailments are for practical purposes nonexistent. If an infirmity affects an individual, it is considered an aberration, which we usually fix within days. Hospitals are no longer needed and have been replaced by Trauma Clinics where we treat injuries caused by accidents.

Inflammations have been contained by the use of vaccines given at birth; as such, appendicitis, cholecystitis, pneumonia, tuberculosis, encephalitis - to name just a few - don't exist any longer; degenerative diseases like arthritis and spondylitis, to name only two of the previous hundred ones, are gone forever; immunological conditions like Crohn's have disappeared through the use of the Anticrohn Globulin. We have defeated psychiatric disorders: depression, anxiety, bipolar disorders, Alzheimer's, Parkinson's and all others have entered the annals of history.

The list of vanished conditions is endless.

The advances in healthcare are such that starting tomorrow my position will not exist. It will be replaced by a Secretary of Pursuing Happiness.

Our conquest has implications in the anthropological, biological, sociological and political spheres. Health care is not impinging on the resources of our nations. Compared to fifty years ago we are dedicating less than three percent of our national budget to Health Maintenance. Income and corporate taxes are now minimal since our expenses are now minimal.

We are all strong, happy and healthy. We have come to accept death as part of a slow deterioration that will impact all of us at different stages of our life. We have made progress and life expectancy stands at 106 years for men and women. What is more important: none of us will die with pain or discomfort. We live without suffering and will die without suffering.

Our vigor may decline - but thanks to the medical advances of the last seventy-five years - later than ever before. Our sex life is the best it has ever been. We live in an environment of joy, an elevated spiritual enjoyment. Sorrow exists but is attenuated by the support we get from society.

Rancor and hatred have been replaced by love, and tranquility took over the chaos of the past. Some of us still remember when long ago, we had to spend an inordinate amount of time caring for our loved ones. This is not needed in the physical sphere because infirmities of old age are easily managed and debilitated states are rapidly reversed.

We owe these accomplishments to the dedicated women and men that over this last century have put all their efforts into eradicating disease; we have achieved the epiphany of the common good.

We did all this, understanding that disease is not caused by external agents but rather by an aggregate of multiple factors, which include noxious agents, environmental elements, and psychosocial components. I must emphasize that these achievements extend all over the world; in the past countries like Bangladesh, Somalia, and others from Asia and the African continents were considered Third World countries, while today there is only one world. There is an interconnection between our wellness and the state of affairs in different areas, as we will learn from the next speakers. The realm of the impossible is today an anecdote. All these accomplishments have been achieved by planning and strategizing; curiously, it was much easier than anticipated 75 years ago. The resources to reach good fortune, prosperity and safety have been present for four centuries; it took the right mindset to achieve our goal.

I would like to encourage the people to read "Bye, bye - The End of Disease as we knew it", a publication of the World Health Organization, which is available in our Virtual Thumb Site (or what was called a website in the past). You may compress the reading from 11 to 2 minutes utilizing the Squeezed Methodology, accessible by entering your name followed by Code: FYI.

My name is Paolo Catena. Starting tomorrow, I will be no longer the Secretary of War of the United Nations; this position will be replaced by the Secretary of Peace. It has now been ninety years since we have witnessed the last war. Since then, there have not been any conflicts between nations. Aggression has been buried in the temple of peace. We don't need to force our enemy to do what we want because there are no enemies. There is no nuclear warfare because there are no nuclear weapons. The extinction of the human species will not be apocalyptic.

Today, for us, it is unconceivable that the World has lived in a state of perpetual warfare until recently. Wars have been explained by von Clausewitz as the need to impose our will on others. Many have considered the state of war as emanating from our human nature - a statement very distant from the truth. It was rather sociological or cultural factors which determined the need to conquer the other. To think that more than 100 hundred million people were casualties of the Second World War is frightening and repugnant at the same time.

Civil wars have ended; warfare is nonexistent.

Cruelty has vanished because despair ceased to exist. The armed forces of all nations now fulfill a sublime mission. They help us control natural catastrophes; they are engaged in modernizing all means of transportation.

We can now reach Tokyo from New York in forty minutes.

Previous civilizations have perpetrated genocide, rape and ethnic cleansing; today this is difficult to comprehend.

At one time Palestinians and Israelis were enemies; Armenians and Turks were foes; Shiites and Sunnis killed each other; Christians crusaded to kill Jews; Croatians fought Serbs; the Irish, the Spaniards and others wanted a homeland of their own, separate from the main territory. These conflicts, to name just a few, would be inconceivable in our era. I am not going to elaborate on why people of different ethnicities did not get along in the past; suffice it to say only that conflict resolution was simple; just as an example, it only took an apology from the Turkish authorities for the Armenians to embrace them as friends.

In the past acts of terrorism have killed and maimed millions of civilians; today they are part of the dark chapters of history.

We don't claim what is not ours; we don't conquer, so nobody has to retreat.

The department of Homeland Security is no longer needed. Many generations ago people boarding a plane had to practically disrobe, take off their belts, shoes and remove all belongings from their pockets. This today is risible and fodder for stand-up comedians.

None of us have to surrender but to the cause of peace and love.

Because of the progress achieved in understanding each other, we have changed the political, philosophical and social equations of the past.

The new paradigm has forced us to change the way we interpret Nietzsche, Spinoza and all other great philosophers. We are no longer inherently violent, if we ever were. Deprivation and its manipulation made people want to die for their country. But now we are one World, one Nation living with fairness and justice for all mankind. When there is Peace, there is no victory and no defeat.

We have extracted from our souls the best we are and the best we can be.

We are certain to presage that there will be no more wars. It will not happen. There are no weapons, no nuclear arms, and no armies - only soldiers of peace. The energy that once we had to fight each other has been channeled to build, create and to love each other.

The artistic craft used to be inspired in the past by angst, suffering, hate, jealousy and other feelings derived from inner dissatisfaction. Today art expresses beauty, love, devotion to others, adoration of nature, attraction between human beings and other things of the heart.

By decree, the Secretary of War will cease to exist immediately. The doors of our new Department of

Peace will be open to everybody, to accept suggestions as how to improve our personal life.

My name is Isidoro Valdetierra. I am the Secretary of Economy of the United Nations and like the previous speakers; I can unambiguously affirm that there is no one single individual that lacks a roof over his head. There are 21 billion people on the planet and about 7 billion families. The combined efforts of our leaders have made it possible that we all can enjoy the coziness of a home. Not only have we achieved habitation for all but we have been able to provide wellbeing to the point that nobody would feel the discomfort that cold or hot weather may bring. This has been achieved by regulating a global economy for a global society. Our common currency, our fair share of resources, the determination of everybody to limit the consumption of goods to what is essential and to regulate the market of the superfluous, have increased our purchasing power to a point that we willingly allocate the surplus to others. This explains how crime has – for all practical purposes – diminished to the point that only passion and questions of the heart are the motivators. The expansion of the economies are no longer unilateral but rather universal; the welfare of the people is the only consideration.

We are on the right path; although we soon are going to enter into the period of deconstruction, all contingencies have been considered.

My name is Richard Lloyd and I have been named Secretary of Deconstruction by the Board of Directors of the United Nations to assure that we depart in a peaceful and laudable transition manner. The word apocalypse has a negative connotation because it denotes destruction, angst, despair and suffering. I would prefer to talk about loving termination.

It is not a catastrophic event that brings us to the end of civilization. On the contrary, we have conquered poverty and disease and have achieved peace to an extent not known previously. The departure will be smooth, without anxiety or disconcert. Nobody will be gone before it is time. There won't be annihilation but rather a slow end. You are all aware that for some unknown reason, five years ago, our reproductive systems ceased to function; paradoxically, animals maintained their biological process intact and we anticipate that their offspring will dominate the Earth. We have discarded any supernatural phenomenon responsible for our condition and we are convinced that an undiscoverable element has altered the biology of reproduction of the human being. We still are coupling with our mates and sex remains as good and pleasurable as always. When we are gone, our children no longer will have children to bear our name. In that sense we are now all Christians, Jewish and Muslims. In that sense we are now all rich and poor. In that sense we are all one. We will die of natural causes and at different times; because of this we have time to leave the world clean, tidy and unpolluted. We are now bonded by this unexpected occurrence and yet even confronting death we care for each other and for the Planet.

I am gathering the best and most brilliant minds to start the process of deconstruction in a way that will not affect the mental or physical capacity of anyone. I am sad and happy at the same time. Sad because there will not be more children and Humanity will cease to exist, but happy because our civilization has achieved for the first time a degree of civility and happiness never seen before.

We don't know what made us males become sterile.

Let's listen to what Seyle Fromm, the renowned scientist, has to say regarding this phenomenon:

Now that we have achieved total comfort and everything is provided to us, without the need to struggle or fight, biologically there is no need to assure the survival of the species.

This is implicit in our calm, unruffled, composed spiritual life. We have become an ocean without *waves, winds without force, suns without glow. It is like light and darkness don't matter any longer. The agitation of times past does not exist.*

We thought that only a cataclysm or a natural catastrophe could bring our civilization to an end.

We never conceived that lack of ambition, the scarcity of goals, the curtailment of aspirations and the easy access to fulfill our desires, would diminish our drive to procreate.

We don't need to fight for our survival; the Government has protected and shielded us from the perils of life. This has made the warrior within us vanish. We love our family and friends but even this love has been substituted by the love that Government has provided. They have given us all we need, food, a roof, and have attended to all our needs. We don't need anybody else to take care of us.

We have no need to fight, because we have no enemies; no need to hunt because we are well nourished; no need to possess because we have enough material objects.

As a consequence the hormones needed for procreation have reached levels that are incompatible with reproduction.

We can depart with no anguish or sorrow.

Friends

My name is Sebastian Epstein. I am seventy years old, a successful businessman. Over the years my circle of friends has declined while my acquaintances have multiplied.

Some of my friends died, others moved to distant places and with others I can no longer connect intellectually or emotionally. I was invested in relationships that lacked reciprocity, with others I could not reconcile our political differences, so I erased them from my life.

My social networking is vast, and yet I cannot confide my feelings, preoccupations or talk about substantial subjects.

At age 12 I was part of gang of four that remained loyal to each other. After graduating from the university, at age 25, we departed to different destinies. One moved to France, one to Seattle and one to Orange County, 55 miles from where I live. We see each other every few years; the quality of our friendship remains strong, perhaps because we don't visit each other very often.

We communicate via e-mails, although this form of contact is not very appealing to me.

Eugene, who lives in France, is an adventurer. He loves scuba diving and he sends me 5 to 6 page-long accounts of his exciting journeys to the most remote parts of the world. He writes very well, his prose is elegant, always adding French words or expressions to his stories. Since I don't exercise at all, because of a bad back, I am very jealous of his escapades.

Joseph is a hypochondriac. He always writes about his imaginary aches and asks us if we would know of any non-traditional solution to his infirmities since none of his eight doctors are able to help him. His last complaint is that of a prick sensation on the lobe of his left ear; he is convinced that it is a manifestation of a brain tumor, although his last three scans have been negative.

Alex is a wealthy real estate investor, sort of a mogul, who loves to inform us about his latest acquisitions; it looks as he owns half of Orange County.

In spite of our differences we are bonded by the affection of the past.

I love them. They are there for me if needed, I guess, but there is a geographical distance that keeps us apart.

Luckily, I have been able to compensate for the lack of a net of pals.

When I was 10 years old I had many imaginary friends who made me happy and full. I could talk, get mad, scream, and bonded intensely with my invented friends. They stayed loyal and unconditional, in contrast with the real ones, with whom we were always squabbling.

One of my friends was Emilio Salgari's Sandokan. With him I fought the Dutch and the British and went to India to fight the Thugs. Together we were invincible. Sandokan shaped my character. I became fearless; there was no enterprise that we couldn't undertake.

Another beloved fantasy friend with whom I shared many adventures was Mark Twain's Tom Sawyer. I identified with him, talked to him, played with him. We shared a passion for Becky, his classmate. We almost drowned in the Mississippi River when we went rafting. The most memorable feature of our relationship was escaping from Joe the killer, through vertiginous caves. Together we were invincible and able to conquer what for others were unconquerable situations.

I never befriended Superman; somewhat his double personality annoyed me. Instead, I preferred Kirby, who became a good companion; together we defeated villains and thieves.

My most fun was introducing my good friend, the Invisible Man, to my five-year-old sister. She would get scared at the idea that there was somebody else in the room that she couldn't see. The Invisible Man was able to do things that all human beings did but he was imperceptible. I could bump into him and my knee would hurt, or talk to him; he would answer only to me. Sis would run and tell my parents that I was playing a frightening game that she did not like. My father, who liked jokes as much as I did, went along with the prank and interacted with our indiscernible guest. Dad pretended that he was drinking his wine and quarreled with him, he would spill some drops from the glass, get mad and at that point my sister would get panicky. My mother would get her arms around my sister and accuse my Dad and me of being foolish and mean.

Those imaginary friends left me when I went to college but now in my old age they are coming back. I have developed a strong emotional attachment and appreciate them more than ever before. They help me in many ways: when I am short of words they come to my rescue, when I have writer's block they come to my help; they give meaning to my thoughts; they are the source of my inspiration.

They are loyal, put no demands on me and when I am tied up by facts or circumstances, they encourage freeing me from those binds.

Without them I will be deprived of my fantasies, I wouldn't travel ethereally to distant lands, I couldn't fulfill my desires, I wouldn't be whole.

My success is their success; my failures are their failures.

Garbanzo Beans

Two nights ago my 14 year old son Frederick asked me what love is. I was about to improvise an answer. Many things came to mind: affection, kinship, passion and others and yet I could not articulate a sensible response.

This morning before going to work, I casually told my wife Annie that I somewhat remember how tasty a dish she used to cook of garbanzo beans mixed with white rice was.

This evening for dinner Annie served a delicious plate of garbanzo beans.

That is what love is.

Global Economy

Los Angeles; 4:14 PM: Automated Response: *You have reached Nespresso, may I have your name?*

Los Angeles; 4:14.18: *My name is Mario*

Philippines; 8:14 AM: Automated Response *–For Customer Service, please press one, for all other inquiries please press two*

Los Angeles; 4:15 PM: Mario *–presses two*

Philippines; 8:15 AM: Automated Response *–for Technical Support press one, for all other inquiries please press two*

Los Angeles; 4:16 PM, presses one

Bombay, India: 5:47 AM: John (his real name is Tagore) *–Hi, my name is John. Thank you for calling Nespresso; how can I assist you today?*

Los Angeles; 4:18 PM: Mario *–I just bought a U Nespresso Machine and it is not dispensing coffee.*

Bombay, India: 5:18 AM: John (Tagore) – *Sorry to hear that. Make sure that the machine is plugged into a main, turn the machine ON by operating the slider, insert a Nespresso capsule and press the touch control once.*

Los Angeles; 4:19 PM: Mario –*OK, I just did but still there is no coffee dripping.*

Bombay, India: 5:20 AM: John (Tagore) – *Sorry to hear that, give me a couple of minutes* (puts Mario on hold while he looks at the manual but cannot come up with a solution). *Sorry for that; let me transfer your call to my supervisor.*

Prague, Czech Republic; 1:27 AM: Dick (his real name is Vaclav) –*Hi, my name is Dick, the Nespresso supervisor; I understand from Mario that you are having problems dispensing coffee. Have you checked that the water tank is filled with water?*

Los Angeles; 4:28 PM: Mario –*You are a genius, Dick, I forgot to fill the tank with water-* fills the tank- *thank you, it is dripping now.*

Prague, Czech Republic; 1:29 AM: Dick (Vaclav) –*You are welcome, if you don't mind, please stay on the line for a brief survey.*

Sucre, Bolivia; 8:30 PM: Peter (his real name is Pedro) –*How would you score our service from 1 to 5, 1 being bad and 5 excellent?*

Los Angeles; 4:31 Mario, savoring and expresso (coffee from Colombia) with sugar (from Brazil), in a cup (made in China) and a silver spoon (from South Africa) – *Quatre- 4 -* (in French).

I am Okay

My friend Rachel F. sent an e-mail to her closest friends announcing what happened to her Uncle Tony.

Tony was in good health. When he was nearing 70, his wife Betty told him to get a check-up since he never had one. Tony was reluctant because he was feeling well. *Precisely,* said Aunt Betty, *prevention starts when you are feeling well and not when you get sick.* So there he went. The doctor gave him a thorough physical examination and ordered a bunch of laboratory tests. He asked him to come back in 10 days to discuss the results.

You are doing fairly well, the doctor told him, *but there are some minor problems. Your blood pressure is in the upper limit of normal, what we call pre-hypertension, and your total cholesterol is normal but the Low Density Lipoprotein, what we call the bad cholesterol, is slightly elevated. So I would like you to take Lipitor and for your blood pressure just 5 mg. of Norvasc. Take also 1 multivitamin in the morning and 4 capsules of Fish*

Oil, and to protect your stomach from these meds take one Prilosec before going to bed.

Tony went to the pharmacy and bought the medications, which he placed in a nice pink pill box with many compartments. A week later he noticed that his ankles were swollen and he also had some pounding heartbeats.

The doctor told him not to worry; the edema and the palpitations were from Norvasc, so he prescribed a diuretic and a small dose of Atenelol.

A couple of weeks later he went to see the doctor again because he was feeling weak, had some insomnia and his muscles were sore.

The doctor examined him and told him not to fret; the soreness was from Lipitor and his insomnia probably from depression so he told him to take Ambien for sleep, Ibuprofen for the soreness and a small dose of Zoloft for depression.

As days passed he was feeling worse and worse. He didn't go out of the house because he was spending all his time taking the medications.

One day he got the flu so Betty gave him chicken soup and called the doctor. With his nice manners he told my aunt not to worry, the flu was caused by a virus so he prescribed Tamiflu and just in case Amoxicillin. After few days he developed a fungus, a known complication in people taking antibiotics, and was given Fluconazole.

Since he was staying in bed most of the time, out of boredom he started reading all the prospects and learned all about warnings, contraindications, side effects and drug interactions. He learned terrible things. He could get heart arrhythmias, gastrointestinal bleeding, nausea, renal insufficiency, diarrhea, constipation and death, among many other things.

He got scared and called his doctor, he told him not to be concerned, that it was routine for the pharmaceutical companies to write in the pamphlets about these kinds of scary things. Before hanging up he advised Tony to double the dose of Zoloft.

His check from Social Security was spent almost entirely to pay for the medications. Weeks passed and he became really sick, could not walk straight, was restless, tired, aching all over and finally died.

Aunt Betty told me that she was grateful to God that she insisted in Tony having a complete check-up; otherwise he would have died several months before.

This story is dedicated to those who take no medications, walk every day or not; drink a glass of red wine a day or more; eat little salt or not; eat refined sugar or not so refined; and eat fat and have sex as often as they like.

In Defense of Literary Fraud and Plagiarism

Most of you probably know me since I am a well recognized literary author, playwright, and theater director. My name is Scott Lithgow. This is not about me, but rather about a subject that concerns several of my good friends. The reader may believe that since they are my friends I am writing about their sorrow and misery, in order to restore their reputation and standing in our society. This is far from my intention. It is not commiseration but an adherence to my principles that makes me debunk the mistaken notion that plagiarism is bad, a ghastly endeavor that should be avoided for those that are in the activity of creation, improvisation and innovation. By extension, literary fraud falls in the same category of plagiarism.

Danny Santiago, a middle aged non-Hispanic gentleman, was dethroned from his literary achievement because he assumed the identity of a young Chicano boy growing in East Los Angeles when he published his acclaimed novel *"Famous All*

Over Town". The fact that he attached a false trait to his persona would not have made any difference to his readership. In a similar circumstance we found James Frey who 'forged' a memoir, *"A Million Little Pieces",* about struggling with drug addiction, although he never used drugs and was not afflicted with an addiction disorder. He was indicted for lying and yet the essence of his praised book remained what it was.

My friend Jonah Lehrer in his superb book that sold 200,000 copies, *"Imagine: How Creativity Works",* fabricated quotes from Bob Dylan in order to make a point about the mechanism by which our imagination works. When it was discovered that his citations were a product of Jonah's imagination, he was forced to resign his prominent position at *The New Yorker.* The book remains a superb treatise about one aspect of our mind. In addition Michael Moynihan, writing in the tablet magazine, accused him of plagiarism in an earlier Lehrer book. *The New Yorker* was concerned about the reputation and integrity of the magazine and gave Lehrer a way out by accepting his resignation. The alternative for the publisher was to show some humility, a better understanding of human nature, elevate itself from the customary politically correct form that is so common in our society, accept Jonah's apologies and move on. That shift in position from *The New Yorker* would have been revolutionary, an implicit acceptance of human frailty and a gesture indicating that the publishers have an innovative and advanced vision of what literature is about.

Recently, my colleague Fareed Zakaria was suspended from CNN and *Time Magazine* for plagiarism.

Fareed is one of the best journalists and thinkers with a significant knowledge of global issues. He writes for *Time Magazine* on a regular basis and hosts a Sunday program on *CNN*. He acknowledged copying material for an article he wrote about gun control from *The New Yorker*. He was sorry, apologized and admitted his mistake as a lapse in judgment. He was clearly repentant for this action. Accepting his apologies was not enough, so castigation ensued.

To all who have the power to reprimand, I would say: if any of us is without sin, let him be the first to throw a stone (here I am plagiarizing Jesus).

American author Jonathan Lethem delivered a passionate defense of the use of plagiarism in art in his 2007 essay "*The Ecstasy of Influence: A Plagiarism*" in *Harpers Magazine.* He wrote, "The kernel, the soul-let us go further and say the substance, the bulk, the actual and valuable material of all human utterances - is plagiarism: and "Don't pirate my editions, do plunder my visions. The name of the game is Give All. You, reader, are welcome to my stories. They were never mine in the first place, but I give them to you" (Disclaimer - just in case - copied and pasted from Wikipedia, so I assume I am not stealing from Mr. Lethem).

We should judge writers, artists, journalists, poets, architects, designers, and all others by the totality of their work. From time to time we all borrow: perspectives, techniques, words, phrases, drawings, musical notes, colors and materials that inspire us to create and to build.

For those that knowingly or unknowingly have allowed me to utilize their material, I thank them. If they are offended I will next time give them the attribution they deserve.

Finally, as the author of this essay I want to make several things clear: my name is not Scott Lithgow; I never met Santiago, Frey, Lehrer, or Zakaria and I intentionally took an artistic license to make my points.

Messi

A Butterfly

That nobody can catch;

A gazelle -

He runs

And runs,

Evasive:

Catch me if you can -

A gambit,

A hat trick,

A penalty kick.

His right foot

Or his left

Or his head -

Chip a shot,

Hide the ball,

And on top

He breaks

The mouth of the goal.

What does Hudson say?

Brilliant,

Like an alligator

With a twitch.

Not a butterfly?

Not a gazelle?

An alligator

Or a lion

A flea,

But with wings.

Supernatural,

Pique says,

Genius

Then;

Genius

Now.

Not a butterfly, an alligator, a lion, a flea,

Not a gazelle -

A new creature:

Lionel.

The Art of Thievery

I am an art expert, a thief and the proud father of five beautiful children. They call me Monsieur Chardon, although I prefer to be called Lucien. I have been married twice, and in serious relationships three times; all my children were from my first wife Gertrude. They all were born in Paris, France.

Gertrude died in childbirth when she was 33 years old. She was the love of my life, gracious and sophisticated and yet exuded humility and simplicity; she had an eternal splendor in her eyes and a perpetual smile.

Our life was full of enjoyment. We shared the love of art, nurtured by my education and on her from instinct and an innate sense to judge form and color better than most of the 'recognized' connoisseurs.

We had a large circle of friends and many acquaintances with whom we spent time and again discussing art, literature and politics.

Those years were the happy times, a period of contentment, in a house full of noise and laughter.

The kids inherited from their mother, a pleasant disposition, a strong character and an unruffled demeanor with the exception of Antoinette, who had a short temper and was never able to hold back when something bothered her.

We lived in a large house, where we worked, played and entertained. We owned 22 pieces of art, collected over a span of 10 years. With the exception of one Manet lithograph, the rest were from amateurs, promising artists, whom we 'discovered' with our good eye.

When I was eighteen years old I applied to the Ecole Nationale Superieure des Beaux-Arts in Paris. I had an intrinsic love for paint and engraving. The conditions for admission were brutal. Candidates were required to ascertain their skills by drawing human models and objects in two settings. On the first, the candidate was to represent them as faithfully as possible; free expression was not accepted. The second part consisted of painting the same objects renouncing fidelity and realism. I passed the first one with flying colors. One of the professors thought that my drawings looked more like photographs. I didn't know whether to take this as a compliment or a critique. During the second part of the entrance examination, I was supposed to use my creativity and imagination. I failed miserably; I could not produce any meaningful piece of art. It appeared that in my case, fidelity was more important than fantasy, yet I was able to judge abstract expressionism, cubism and other forms of representations from others, better than most. I was patted on my back by the Dean of the School, Monsieur Granier, and dismissed with some words of solace. 'It is fine Lucien, don't feel bad; remember that we also refused entrance to our school to Rodin on three different occasions.'

I accepted my fate and enrolled in Art Studies at the Sorbonne; at the end of my education, I became an art critic. I worked for Le Monde and became well respected. My reviews and critiques always included explanations about the subtleties and nuances of a painting or a sculpture without using pompous or difficult language. My reviews were considered sanctimonies. I never offended anyone; more than once I refused a bribe from art dealers, who wanted me to embellish an artist.

My life was good; the children added spice to our existence. Each one had a different personality: Pierre was strong and determined and assumed the responsibility of being the older brother, defending his siblings with ferocious resolve, from the not infrequent malice of other kids. Claude was a free spirit with a short attention span and although this could have been a handicap, it was compensated by his talents; with little dedication he managed to excel. Berthe was pretty, shy and intelligent, Antoinette the most creative of them all.

Then, in one day, everything was interrupted; an unmerciful death showed all its power, taking the life of Gertrude the same day that life came for Annie.

My despair became untamed. I could not work nor rest. My senses became numb; my enthusiasm for life was gone. My sister Marianne took care of the children; I was submerged in a cloud of never-ending sadness. This period lasted almost one year; then little by little the forces of despair started fading away. When I became myself again, I went back to Le Monde to claim my old job, but a younger art critic had taken my place. In a short time he became famous and acclaimed, feared by many artists. I was assigned a temporary position in the Art and Leisure section of the newspaper. My demotion was painful and unsavory. Before my absence I was treated with admiration and deference; when I came back occupying a lesser position, my co-workers treated me with coziness and impertinence, I became one of them, no longer Lucien Chardon, the acclaimed art critic.

I did not enjoy my new assignment but I needed a job to support my five children. I gathered strength to pull forward, hoping that happy days would come back again.

Seven years passed.

One day I was introduced to Marie Claire, a pretty girl who was 10 years younger than me. We dated for one year. My relation with Marie Claire was good; sex was good, although the passion that nourished my life with Gertrude was not there. My sister insisted that I should get married, out of respect to my household.

One year into our marriage, as I was having coffee at Le Deux Magots with my friend Philippe, we saw Marie Claire walking by, holding hands with a young man of about her age. That night I asked her about her whereabouts, she responded with a lie. Weeks passed; it became clear that she was becoming emotionally detached from me and the kids. The culmination of our marriage came peacefully, without screams or recriminations. The departure was civilized, albeit painful.

Again, life became dull, nothing interested me anymore.

One evening I was visiting a show of Post-impressionists at the Zibron Gallery. One painting was Paul Cezanne's *View of Auvers-sur-Oise.* This was my preferred Cezanne; I admired the intensity of the brush-strokes and the depiction of a never-ending swirling green landscape. That night I could not sleep; I felt the urge to possess the piece. Suddenly, I felt alive and experienced an excitement long gone. The sense of anticipation and certainty, that somehow, I was going to seize the Cezanne, changed my whole existence. I became cheerful and buoyant; once again I was the master of my life.

It was time to take action. The show was going to end in 11 days and I had to devise a plan that would need careful preparation. I paid a visit to the Gallery two more times. During the first one I located the fuse box, which was in a closet adjacent to the manager's office. I opened it and rapidly identified the alarm switch. During my second visit I injected a silicon paste into the two padlocks from the back door and retrieved them within two minutes. With the two molds I manufactured the keys that would allow me to gain access to the showroom. The final step entailed the distraction or the containment of the security guard. During my previous visit, I noticed that he was armed, so I decided to bring a taser gun to paralyze him, if needed. I elected to execute the plan in the early hours of July 14; being a holiday the city would be at a standstill. At two o'clock in the morning I entered the premises, went directly to the fuse box, turned the alarm off and quietly proceeded to the main salon and with a pair of pliers removed the Cezanne from its place. The guard was napping in a chair and so there was no need for further action; I left as quietly as I entered.

The robbery was considered a masterful action. None of the detectives assigned to the case could explain how it was perpetrated. They construed that two or three persons entered the Gallery, without forcing the lock, so they decided that it probably was an inside job. They subjected the 10 employees of the Gallery to a lie detector test;

everybody passed with the exception of the manager; yet he could not be convicted on the basis of the test alone; he had an alibi, having spent the entire night with his lover, a young Parisian lad by the name of James. The security guard claimed that he never fell asleep, heard no noise or for that matter did not notice anything suspicious. He stated that he probably was taking a bathroom break when the piece was removed from the wall.

View of Auvers-sur-Oise had a price tag of 10 million Euros. I did not rejoice at the price, but rather at my accomplishment. I did not feel guilty, nor have any regrets, and I did not share my accomplishment with others.

I became a changed man. I was no longer taciturn or sad; my zest for life came back again. I had no immediate plans to sell the painting.

And again in one day, my life changed again.

It was on a Friday afternoon; Annie insisted I go with her to Galleries Lafayette to renew my wardrobe. I have been using the same clothes for years and years. I dislike shopping and have a pathological aversion to those megashops. I usually develop an agitation that makes me leave after 20 minutes or so. Nevertheless, knowing Annie, I knew I could not refuse. The place was crowded; the displays of merchandise were in bad taste. I wondered why the place was so popular. While my daughter was trying to match ties and shirts, I noticed three Japanese kids about the ages of 6 and 9, hiding and playing carelessly between the racks of clothing. Then a beautiful slender woman with dark hair and bronzed skin approached them and softly talked to them, probably warning them to be careful. She was not talking to them in French, but I could not recognize the language because of the surrounding noise. I assumed that she knew them, then the mother of the kids appeared and told them to quiet down; they talked for a while, and then after few minutes the mother and the kids left.

I assumed that the dark-haired woman spoke Japanese, and when we crossed paths, I candidly asked her where she learned to speak Japanese. She looked at me, smiled and then laughed. I felt embarrassed and apologized. She commented how perceptions lead people to reach false presuppositions. In fact, she was talking to the Japanese kids in Spanish. That family was visiting from Peru, where they lived. I may have blushed and she corresponded by blushing herself. "By the way," I said, "my name is Lucien"; she responded, "Maria Saavedra." We initiated a conversation. Saavedra was her second name and not a surname, she was French, her parents were born in Spain. At that time Annie came with her bounty of shirts and ties and pants; I made a formal introduction.

After few minutes I looked at Maria and knew that I was falling in love, just like that - in a split second. Things from the heart are undecipherable.

Annie had the intuition of something happening and discreetly disappeared. We chatted and when it was time to depart I asked Maria Saavedra if she would like to join me for sushi, since Japan was responsible for our encounter. She told me that dinners were not good for her, but she would be happy to have lunch some other day. That is how things started. We met several times for lunch or coffee, never for dinner. She learned about my life, and I about hers.

She was a psychoanalyst with a busy practice. She was a 'Lacanian', after Jacques Marie Lacan, and applied his teaching principles in her practice; she came to appreciate not only his analytical techniques, but the value of being eclectic. After all Lacan renewed his alliance with Freud after having a period of fights and quarrels; nothing was fixed in the Universe. At the beginning we became good friends, I had to set aside my declaration of love for reasons that I didn't know. I touched her hand frequently but she avoided mine. Yet our eyes were speaking words what we couldn't utter. I wanted her, but felt there was a barrier which was better not to cross.

One day after an animated encounter, we were walking toward her office and without saying a word, she kissed me. I hugged her, held her close to me, clinched for minutes. We became unbound.

Later, I learned that Maria Saavedra was in a struggling relationship. As she was becoming more attracted to me, she had held back her feelings out of a sense of loyalty to Jacques, her conflicting lover. Betraying and deceiving were not part of her makeup. The night previous to our entanglement she had broken the relationship. The next day, she felt free to do what she wanted to do for a long time.

I invited her to have breakfast in my apartment the next morning. The previous night I could not sleep because of a feeling of anticipation.

I prepared a luscious meal but that morning we did not have breakfast; as soon as she entered the room we kissed, embraced, and cuddled, then stripped and made love. She was in command; she would hold me tight when she wanted to slow my thrust, even as I was still palpitating inside of her. She would run her fingers over my spine and I would feel an exhilaration that I never experienced before. Our bodies twirled, we explored each other and promised to become lovers forever.

I admired her intellect. She would interpret and give meaning to simple life deeds, to relationships between people, or elaborate in the covert meaning of a political discourse.

The day previous to our first encounter, she had been an expert witness in a case where a young woman was being convicted of a crime on the basis of one single eyewitness, who recognized her in a police lineup. Maria explained to the judge and jurors the dynamic of misperceptions. She showed them the classic two straight lines with inner or outer v shapes at each end, and everybody agreed – having been privy to this test before – that they were equal. In fact, Maria had made one longer than the other by several centimeters, but bias made them reach the wrong conclusion; on the basis of this simple demonstration, the defendant was exonerated.

When I met her in Gallery Lafayette I imagined that she was talking Japanese to the kids, another example of a long list of misperceptions; that was why she laughed, the laugh that got me entrapped.

My work at Le Monde was becoming more disappointing. I was to write what my editors decided and not what I wanted, so in an impromptu act, I tendered my resignation. A few days later I began to doubt if, at my age, with still some financial obligations, I had done the right thing. Maria Saavedra was very supportive; I felt totally free.

One day, Gustave, a good a friend of mine, who was the Director of a Heart Institute in Saint-Denis, asked me if would be willing to give a lecture on Impressionism at his Clinic. Every

Wednesday the eight doctors working there would have lunch, prepared by Gustave, who was an excellent amateur cook. During the meal they would invite a guest speaker to talk about different subjects. I gave a lecture for 20 minutes and took questions for another 20. For this I was paid 1000 Euros. The meeting was very enjoyable, and went better than expected.

So that was how my new occupation started. I became a well paid art lecturer for the well-to-do. An article in ELLE praised me as a rare talent, an educator who could convey, in simple ways, the meaning of art.

After a while, boredom set in. I was living a good life, my five kids were independent, all accomplished in what they were set to do, Pierre was about to get married, Antoinette was in a lasting, cheery relationship with Louise, a ballet dancer, and I was blissful to have Maria Saavedra as my sweet companion. We both maintained our residences, which were two subway stations away from each other, somewhat this arrangement made our encounters more exultant.

During one day of intense ennui, I decided to do something to shake my tedium. Alas! I knew what to do; it was time to sell my beloved *Auvers-sur-Oise*. The river would still be flowing, even if I renounced the painting. Maria noticed my exhilaration and did not know why, but accepted it as one of the churning waves of the spirit.

My plan required setting a price for the painting, finding a buyer and having the money transferred to a bank account. The major obstacle to this transaction was finding somebody willing to buy this very expensive piece of art.

I remembered that five years ago Ari, the owner of an antique shop in Reims, was suspected to be the intermediary in the sale of a stolen Rubens, but he was never convicted.

This was going to be a good place to start. I arrived in the city in a warm day. I crossed Place d'Erlon where people sitting outside were enjoying the summer sun; around the corner was Ari's shop. It had an innocuous façade, in contrast with the interior, which was filled with sculptures, paintings, vases, jewelry and whatever satisfies lovers of objects from distant pasts. I was greeted by a young handsome fellow with Greek factions. I engaged in casual conversation with this vivacious and talkative young man. He introduced himself as George Andropoulos, the owner's son. He called his father, who was in the upstairs office. Ari was a big, husky guy who, although calm and poised, never smiled. What struck me the most was that as soon as he appeared, George became withdrawn and lost his previous cheerful demeanor.

I asked Ari to retire to more private quarters; we moved up to his office, which contrary to my expectations – there is my bias again – was immaculate and clean. There was a sleek computer on the desk and a pencil holder, no papers, crowded folders or books. There were two clean upholstered comfortable chairs, and on the walls one *Petter Hegre* and one *Sonia Noskowiak* photograph. I introduced myself and asked Ari to do two things: one, to read my Bio in Wikipedia and two, to go over a file I brought with newspaper clips about the theft of a famous Cézanne. I told him that I would come later that afternoon to discuss a confidential matter.

I strolled though the city, visited Notre-Dame de Reims, learned that the kings of France were once crowned there and after admiring its fine tapestries and *Chagall's* stained glass, went back to Ari's. George was there and his father up in the office with one of his providers. While I was waiting, I asked George about his background. He was, as I had been in my youth, interested in becoming an artist and just like me, he was dismissed by Reims Art School, with a perfunctory 'not good enough'. So, at his father's insistence he got a degree in Business Administration; as an only child he was one day to inherit the lucrative family business. He painted and wrote poetry as a hobby. Our cordial, animated conversation was interrupted by his father, who was coming down with his client. I noticed again that George shut off almost immediately when his dad appeared.

I went up to the office, sat down in a comfortable leather chair and had a short chat with Ari. He was impressed with my bio and told me that he did not need to read the folder I brought; he was well acquainted with the *Cezanne's* disappearance. "Ari, I am going to be brief and to the point, I want you to get me a buyer for the Cezanne; you will keep 25 percent of the proceedings. Don't tell me now if you are going to do it or not. Here is my telephone number; call me only if you want to do it." Then I left.

Two weeks later Ari called and asked me to meet him at Maceo's for lunch. Ari was a vegetarian; each time he came to Paris he indulged with a luscious meal which he could not get anywhere else. He took his time before discussing business. Only when the coffee and cognac arrived, he told me that he had sent George to Moscow to discuss the 'acquisition' of the painting with Mikhail Tzordoski, the Russian tycoon who owned a large collection of art. Mikhail was a patron of the arts and had one of the largest collections of French and Russian paintings displayed in his London and Moscow apartments and in his yacht *Laguna*.

The operation was going to be safe; if he were not to pay or play any trick with us, a letter kept in a safe was going to emerge indicating the whereabouts of the painting and a detailed disclosure of the transaction. The price was going to be 8 million Euros, 5 for me and 3 for Ari. The painting was to be delivered to the *Laguna*, which would be waiting in Marseille. There, Mikhail, two art experts and George were going to ride the yacht for as long as needed to authenticate the painting, after which time, if OK, the money was going to be released. I was to bring the canvas rolled into a tube, wait for George at the port while he was finishing the transaction, split the money as convened; after which time we were not to see each other ever again.

I despised Marseille; twenty years ago I had a belligerent confrontation with a local artist at l'Estaque, the artist colony, about a minor matter, that gave me a major annoyance. This time, I was in the city for business; feelings did not matter. I met George at the New Port. He did not show any sign of apprehension, in contrast with my trepidation and dread for a situation over which I had no control. I handed over the precious cargo; he walked to the pier and disappeared under the fog.

I waited four hours until George emerged again, this time carrying two pieces of luggage, one for me and one for them. My angst did not vanish since the operation was not finished. I drove from Marseille to Monaco, checked at the Hermitage Hotel, took a shower, tried to sleep - a futile attempt - and by 10 o'clock the next day I went to Fortis Bank and deposited the money in an account that I had opened four weeks earlier. Only then was I able to relax and enjoy the French Riviera, with all its beauty.

I returned to Paris; little by little life went on at a calm, predictable pace.

Occasionally I would reflect about my actions; why I would risk my livelihood with such illegal actions was not easy to explain. Clearly it was not the money; I had a life of comfort without luxuries. I knew that if caught, I would have to spend many years in jail, away from my family and losing Maria Saavedra, and yet I had this compulsion to possess art. I could not tame my want. Before my decision to steal the *Cezanne* I was depressed, in constant turmoil. Only after my successful pursuit I became the old Lucien, full of dynamism and an indomitable inner force.

If I could explain why Steve Fossett took the risk of flying solo nonstop around the world in a fixed-wing aircraft, which culminated with his death, or why mountain climbers put their lives in peril trying to reach higher peaks, only then I could understand what I did. In some cases adventures end in death; mine could end with incarceration. And yet the *Cezanne* theft relieved me from my internal demons.

I used the money from my Monaco account sparingly, for gifts to my children or taking trips with Maria to different parts of the world. I continued to delight wealthy people with my teachings about art.

I enjoyed and abhorred my job as an art instructor, depending on the audience. With Gustav and his colleagues it was a delight. They worked as doctors, yet they had the intellectual curiosity to understand an abstract world, which appeared to be far removed from them. They were the last remnants of times gone, when doctors were identified as humanists and lovers of art and literature.

One evening, I received a phone call from Regis Letelier, the owner of the winery that bears his name, inviting me to a dinner session at his place in Passy to enlighten his guests.

Letelier's home exuded warmth and beauty; it laid on a park-like rolling ground. Before dinner, a musical trio played baroque music. Dinner was served by two waiters and a maid, Adele. We savored an excellent meal. There were 12 guests; after dinner we went to a room where his collection of art was gathered. Regis just bought Rembrandt's *The Storm on the Sea of Galilee*, the only seascape that the artist painted, where he depicted Jesus and his twelve disciples and a fourteenth person, probably a self-portrait of Rembrandt. This painting was going to be the center of my presentation.

Before retiring from the dining room, Regis gave a short speech welcoming his guests, introduced me and asked Adele to bring in Camille, the cook who was the artifice of the banquet. She received deserved praise for her deeds. There was a quiet and polite applause; after that we rolled into the art quarters.

I made, as customary, a 20 minute presentation, knowing that the attention span of people attending a conference or speech cannot take longer without risking boredom; when I opened the meeting for questions, it took me only minutes to realize that this audience was a bunch of snobs, with no understanding or appreciation of art. I endured their stupid comments, all directed to brag about a knowledge that they did not possess. They talked for the sake of wanting to be noted.

Several days later, in the middle of the night, I woke up with thoughts that provoked a feeling of enthrallment, which I had experienced once before. I discarded these thoughts during the day; they recurred during the night. I was to possess the Rembrandt, no matter what.

It was foolish to gamble my fate for something that I did not need; yet my urge did not dissipate.

I spent the following weeks devising a plan to possess the Rembrandt. My first task was to study the grounds of the Letelier state, which I did by getting the public record from the title company when the property was bought 15 years before. There was a park-like front yard of about half an acre, a smaller backyard with a swimming pool and on the left the maid's quarters adjacent to a garage where Adele and Camille lived. There were a gardener and a chauffeur attending the house but they did not live on the premises. The Leteliers took frequent business and pleasure trips during the year; they had a home in Cape Cod to escape the heat of the Parisian summers. Adele had

Thursdays and Saturdays off and Camille Wednesday and Sundays. Wednesday evenings, she attended a cooking class at the famous L'Atelier des Sens; otherwise, she spent her time with her sister and nieces who lived in the outskirts of Paris. For the second stage of my plan, I acquired posters and books depicting *The Storm on the Sea*, bought a canvas and reproduced the Rembrandt paint with astonishing fidelity.

Finally, I called George Andropoulos and asked to meet. He was surprised since we had agreed not to talk to each other again. He was coming to Paris for a business meeting, so we decided to meet at Café Angelique for coffee.

He remained the same cheerful, jovial fellow I met a few years ago. He had grown his hair longer and that made him look more handsome. I told him that I wanted to share profits with him on a 50-50 basis in a new 'assignment'.

I explained my plan to seize the Rembrandt. We had to gain easy access to Letelier's mansion. This could be accomplished by him becoming acquainted with Camille. On Thursdays Adele, the other help, had her day off and Camille was alone in the house. After first gaining Camille's confidence, George would then have to gain access to the mansion; once there he would have to make sure that the front and kitchen entrances were going to be unlocked, thus permitting me to enter the house and replace *The Storm on the Sea* with my reproduction. I was going to unframe the original and then make the change. I had rehearsed and timed this task; it was going to take 21 minutes; George had to keep Camille away from the house for at least half an hour. George listened to my words attentively; when I finished, without a hint of hesitation, he extended his hand and nodded his head as a sign of approval.

George enrolled at the L'Atelier des Sens for Wednesday cooking classes. There he 'casually' met Camille. After few encounters George and Camille became lovers. They appeared to be truly happy and she had no hint of the deceit that was going to fall upon her. George learned that the Leteliers were going to be away the first week in August. We decided to carry on the operation that first Thursday, when Adele had her day off. George was to phone Camille at 6 o'clock that evening and tell her that he needed to talk to her right away; as she could not get away and leave the house alone, she would invite George to come to the house.

The day came, and as expected Camille got the call, went to the gate, and greeted George, trembling with anticipation: was he going to propose? They leisurely walked around the park holding hands. They went to Camille's bedroom, removed their clothes, embraced and made love like never before. They became mesmerized by the intensity of their pleasure, and the night became endless.

I accomplished my mission. It was easier than expected. The operation was a success. When Regis and his wife came back from their trip back, they did not notice that the Rembrandt had been switched; life went on as usual.

 I kept the Rembrandt in a vault. George and I decided to wait three months and then offer the piece to Mikhail Tzordoski. George also knew of other potential buyers, but we preferred to deal with Mikhail, a known entity.

One cold winter day, I received an envelope without stamps or a return address, marked Confidential. It read:

My Dear Lucien: What a delight it has been to meet you. You may not believe it, but singlehandedly you have been responsible for changing my life. You have inspired me to be who I am today. I recognized that if Lucien Chardon, the learned art teacher, the essence of good taste and good manners, was able to live the life of others by robbing them of their possessions, something other than dishonesty, greed or voracity could make certain people do what very few people dare to do. When my dad Ari robbed the Rubens our relationship changed forever. Before, we were more than father and son, we were friends, shared the love of art and music and had a kind of affection that only Greeks can have. My mother died a week after the scandal. Dad could not be proven guilty or innocent, but Mom knew and her grief took her away from us. After that day my dad became detached from me. I thought that it was a temporary situation going to revert, as time passed I noticed that although he was his self with others, with me he remained aloof and distant. He could not tolerate my jois de vivre, my zest for life and as you may have noticed, in his presence I became other than who I was. I was surprised that he accepted your proposition and asked me to be the executor of the deed. I thought that perhaps that would bring us back together, but that did not happen. I lived with him and around him with a constant feeling of guilt for a sin that I did not commit. Was I culpable of what? Did he steal the Rubens on my behalf? Or was the muse of Art, the force that transformed his spirit and took him to a vertiginous road with no clear end? Is it the exaltation of our senses that collides with our reason? Who knows? And do we care? We are not ordinary thieves. We may be called robbers by others; are we? I refuse to elaborate further because I am now a happy lad.

I am here with my sweet Camille about to open a French restaurant in a distant land; we are doing this with passion.

But I am missing the point, I am writing to you out of a deep affection and to warn you to be careful, very careful. I will explain. That August 6, you entered Letelier's home swiftly. You gained access to the gallery through the kitchen that was left open. Your manual skills allowed you to dismantle the Rembrandt and replace it with your copy in exactly 19 minutes. You left happy, with a sense of achievement, that I am certain continues up to today. Keep that feeling for the rest of your life: you accomplished what you wanted to do. But make sure not to try to sell the Rembrandt because it is not a legitimate one; rather a copy that I reproduced, hanged in Letelier's room and you took believing it was the original one. In a way I am proud that a connoisseur like you could not recognize that the painting was a fake. Perhaps it was because your judgment was overridden by the anxiety of the moment.

I later told Regis Letelier, of course without naming names, about the replacement; we negotiated the return of the original – for exactly half of its cost (your 50%) - with the condition that he should not report the situation to the police and would not investigate anybody inside or outside the premises. He consented, and when the transaction was finished Camille, who was never a suspect, got the call to join me in my new habitat. By now, it should be obvious to you, that she has been involved in this from the very beginning and this made your masterful plan easy to be accomplished.

My love for Camille was never faked and cannot be reproduced; it will be with us forever.

Lucien, stay well and out of trouble

Your friend always, George

Historical Quiz

Test your knowledge:

Answers below

I did not have sexual relations with that woman

    a.- Bill Clinton. President of the United States

    b.- Thomas Jefferson. President of the United States

I did not use cocaine

    a.- Thomas Edison. Inventor

    b.- Rob Ford, Toronto, Canada Mayor

I did not cheat on my spouse

    a.- Francesca de Rimini (Divine Comedy)

    b.- Arnold Schwarzenegger (Actor and Governor of California)

I did not seek a homosexual encounter

    a.- Larry Craig. United States Senator

    b- Oscar Wilde. English author

I did not expose my genitals to the public

    a.- Anthony Wiener. United States Congressman

    b.- Aphrodite. Greek Goddess of Love and Beauty

Answers

All of them are correct. This illustrates that sex scandals may not be scandals after all, but an integral constituent of the human fabric.

If Presidents, actors, mythological figures, inventors, fictional characters, politicians, and writers have engaged in these 'debauched ' acts, maybe they are not wicked or morally wrong. Depravity may be in the eye of the beholder.

The Carriage

I have been pulling a carriage in Central Park for 12 years. My boss Giovanni died about one year ago. Giovanni came from Sicily with his widow father and seven siblings when he was 10 years old. The family first lived in Staten Island, and then settled in Queens. His father remarried and Giovanni went to live with his aunt Sophia and his uncle Salvatore, who had no children. Giovanni was a quiet, happy chap with no high life ambitions. When he finished primary school he helped another uncle in his shoe repair shop and saved enough money to buy a horse-drawn carriage with a municipal license from a fellow Italian, who was moving back to Catania. The open coach was beautiful, well kept and light enough to put little burden on me and before me, other horses. One lovely evening, as we were wrapped by a gentle breeze and delighted with the sounds of chirping birds, Giovanni dropped dead. I am sure that it was a happy death; his demise occurred while he was riding the carriage that he loved so much.

I remember that day very well. We were at the end of one trip, reached 6th Avenue and took our place in the lineup when he had a sudden heart attack. The young couple riding with us noticed that something was wrong as Giovanni was gasping for air. They summoned a police car that was passing by; an ambulance arrived four minutes later. The commotion was out of the ordinary, at least for me. Sirens sounding all over the air, three police cars had their roof lights blinking; two fire trucks arrived after the ambulance, the Emergency room of the nearest hospital was put on high alert. It was too late. Giovanni never had so much attention in his life - what an irony, when he was alive nobody seemed to care about this good man and then in one split second he got the interest of so many. In spite of their efforts my boss was gone, just like that. The tourists took pictures of the gruesome scene with their cameras. Two days later he was paid homage by *The New York Times* which posted a picture of the carriage, Giovanni and me, Dino, his loyal horse.

Something peculiar happened that evening after Giovanni was carried away. The evening went back to normal; I waited and waited for somebody to take me to the stable but nobody came. After a while, I knew that it was my time to leave Central Park. The road to the stable was one that I have walked many times before. Slowly, with resolved pace, I reached the stable. Lionel and Justin were there as usual. They gently took me away to my stall, disrobed me of my harness and fed me my usual meal, something I always considered a reward for my efforts.

The next day, at seven o'clock, a new crew arrived at the lot and started their routine. They brushed me, fed me and attached me to the carriage. Then they left, probably expecting Giovanni to come and start our daily ride. I suspect that they didn't know that he was gone. Since I was already dressed up and the gates were open I left and went off to the Park. I stopped at every red light, yielded to pedestrians and in less than forty minutes reached my destination.

It was a day with no clouds and a warm temperature. There was a festive mood in the air for no good reason. The green from the park looked greener and luscious; the glass windows from the high rise buildings glimmered.

As I was waiting by the curb, a young couple climbed into the back seat, They didn't notice that the driver was missing or expected him to come at any time; I knew better, so I started my routine and took them to visit the usual highlights of the city. They were enmeshed in themselves not noticing the surroundings; they probably were in their honeymoon. They kissed and embraced. Our ride lasted the customary thirty minutes, when we arrived back to the park they left 90 dollars on the driver's seat and left.

I didn't have to wait that long.

After a while a young mother with her two kids looked at the carriage and then at me. I nodded and swirled my head into the direction of the passenger's seats, they climbed up and I started the ride at my usual pace. They were having a great time. The children were laughing; the mother was cheerful; as a gesture of good will I decided to prolong the trip for another 20 minutes.

I made six more trips that day; I am certain that Giovanni would have approved of my work; I was more diligent than ever, followed the routine as if he was still there and in command. When the time came to go home I drove back to the stable. Lionel and Justin took care of me, removed the harness, fed me, washed me and got me ready for the next day.

The next day, again back to Central Park; I completed all the rides; rituals never die. The routine was repeated day after day.

During the summer, if it was too hot, Lionel would not allow me to go out and I rested in the stable with the other horses.

During the winter Justin provided blankets, that he placed in the back seat to warm our clients.

That is the simple life of a horse and his carriage.

I was surprised that nobody had noticed that there was no coachman but assumed that when we were riding, people didn't notice because they were overwhelmed by the scenery, the grass, the trees, the beauty of the Conservatory Garden, the Bow Bridge, the colors of the Carousel.

Those times were amusing and exciting for my clients and for me.

I came to believe that my carriage was the place where everything can be forgotten. I never heard people discussing politics or money matters, just stuff of the heart.

One day a grumpy old man could not find a taxi and so jumped into the backseat and asked to be taken to 42nd Street. That was not part of my itinerary, so I could not oblige. I remained still, and the man grew impatient. He realized that there was no driver and so jumped out of the carriage, but not before cursing me and the entire city of New York. When he was in the sidewalk, a couple got in and I started riding slowly, as was my style. Donald (that was the name of the grumpy guy) noticed that we rode the road. When I came back to let my passengers get off, Donald was hiding behind a tree. A while later I took one lady for a trip, when I arrived at my spot, Donald had called a journalist friend of his, from the *Post,* waiting for my arrival. He was the first to discover that the carriage was being driven without a coachman.

The *NYP* published an article in their front page; the title read 'Miracle in the Park'; they try to explain in anthropological terms how a horse can drive his carriage all alone and around the city without anybody noticing. The news traveled all over the country and the world. If Central Park was ever a tourist attraction, it was now pandemonium. Everybody wanted to ride with the phenomenal, astounding carriage that rode without a driver. Donald, who happened to be a nasty businessman, managed to take possession of what never was his and charged 333 dollars for a 20 minute ride; before he unearthed reality I was working 8 hours a day, now to satisfy demand, no less than 12.

I did not like these new arrangements, became gloomy and miserable; the whole situation became distressing. One day, after I learned that Donald was going to sell 90 percent of his interest in my carriage to a group of Chinese entrepreneurs, I decided to take action.

It was a Monday morning, the splendor of the day appeared perpetual, nature was harmonic, the weather was superb and the landscape was brighter than ever. Donald invited Mr. and Mrs. Chin, the potential buyers, to jump into the carriage for a solo trip and he gave the order to start the voyage. I looked at Donald and cringed when I saw his big smile; at that moment I knew what I had to do. I stalled. The world came to a standstill; the photographers, the crowd, everybody got startled and did not know how to react. When I did not move all the people but one cheered my action. The ride was over forever. I am sure that Giovanni would have approved.

The Cupcake Syndrome

The Book of Mormon, the praised musical show, has been making the rounds in a lot of cosmopolitan cities in the US; the show usually is sold out for months. It received excellent reviews from acclaimed critics and became a frequent subject of conversation. The screenplay, the music and the performances were commended almost unanimously. Witty, funny, intelligent, creative, realistic, brilliant, daring - those were the words used to describe the show.

I went to see it with high hopes, rejoiced with exhilaration, expecting to see one of those rare performances that come once in a decade.

I didn't like it!

The score was original, which doesn't make it necessarily good; irreverent - always a fresh of good air- but only occasionally funny. The screenplay is a combination of comical and not so comical themes: maggots in the scrotum, clitorectomy, AIDS, paganism, poverty, cruelty, vanity and the triumph of the underdog; a concoction that left a sour taste in my mouth. Were we supposed to take this satire seriously?

I was in a minority or perhaps part of a silent majority that kept their opinions to themselves, to avoid appearing to be counter to mainstream.

Then was time for reflection:

There are many other occurrences of universal acceptance of certain phenomena:

Fifty Shades of Grey is one of those. This is an erotic novel that depicts love scenes of dominance and sadomasochism in abundance. It has been read by millions and has been on the best seller list of the New York Times for many months. This book is a piece of crap, violent, offensive, and not well written. Grey has a pathetic emotional and psychological disorder and the heroine Anastasia is pitiable for allowing Grey to chastise her. I am not making a moral judgment nor am I a prurient fellow, revolted by explicit sex scenes. It is the content that I found disgusting. By the way, it has sold more than 70 million copies worldwide!

These two instances, and thousands like these, make us accept facts or ideas without reviewing them critically. Wanting to be like everybody else, we accept the reviews as absolute truths, either out of ignorance, internal needs or foolishness. By doing so our judgment becomes blurry.

Our instincts, feelings and perceptions are overridden by what others have suggested.

By imitating others we become the others.

Not too long ago, a cupcake bakery, Sprinkles, opened in Beverly Hills. Soon, it became a national phenomenon. Long lines of people wait patiently to savor the small round cakes and after hours there is an ATM-like-machine to dispense them. The cupcakes may be good, but no better than hundreds of others, which have not inspired the same craze.

In Los Angeles there is a legendary hot dog stand, called Pink's Hot Dog. The place is open until 2 or 3 in the morning; no matter the day or the time, waiting lines are non-ending. Their chili dog is as good and as bad as the ones from most eateries; yet Pink's stands alone as a sublime place to eat junk food.

There are legions of restaurants where the lines are well-known and celebrated; some endure, while others quickly disappear.

There is a handbag called Birkin that sells for 9,000 to 150,000 dollars (a handbag, not an automobile!) and there is a waiting list of six months before they commiserate and sell it to you. This purse is a sign of social status (*Darling, I have to have it*) and also of foolhardiness; an inanity that does not deserve further comments.

There is an explanation why we crave.

In psychology it is called cognitive dissonance. It says,: the more difficult and painful it is to get something, the more we want it and the more we like it.

If it takes weeks to get a reservation in a restaurant, once you go there, no matter how the food tastes, you will praise it, either because you lack taste buds or because since you have waited for such a long period, you rationalize that it has to be good. Admitting that you were duped is a worse alternative.

This explains why we are willing to be one of many staying in line for hours to get a new iPad or an iPhone, even if the ones we have are functioning perfectly well.

Imitating or subscribing to the ideas or acts of others may be inconsequential, but when it is a repetitive pattern it becomes a behavioral dysfunction.

This peculiarity of our conduct, if repeated enough, becomes pathological.

The American Psychiatric Association *Diagnostic and Statistical Manual of Mental Disorders,* known by the trade as DSM-IV, is used by clinicians and researchers to categorize patients into a specific diagnosis, reached by consensus by experts in the field. This helps in the study and treatment of people with various mental disorders. Those diagnoses are classified according to severity into mild, moderate and severe. There are hundreds of conditions listed in the manual.

Today I am proposing a new Syndrome. The persistent search for gratifications through the prism of others is now a cultural trait and although innocuous when becoming a repetitive pattern becomes a pathological medical entity: The Cupcake Syndrome, a better option than admitting how stupid we can be.

A Detective Story

I was forced to retire as a detective from the Seattle Police Department because of my age, an obtuse measure that has been in place for decades. Isn't simple logic that one may be 70 and sharp and witty or 50 and dim-witted?

Being a man in law enforcement I had no alternative but to respect the law, which doesn't mean that this and some others are not ill-conceived. As a consequence the city is starved of smart, intelligent detectives like myself.

My colleagues recognized that I, Pepe, as they call me (from Peter Perez, my real name), singlehandedly, had resolved the three most famous crimes in the State of Washington, all of which are now legendary; they have been excerpted in magazines, newspapers and in the Dolphin Case, made into a movie, in which I am a consultant. During the filming I had an opportunity to meet Robert De Niro, who will play me; he is quite a character. He is always joking and showing a nonchalant attitude. My detective instinct tells me that behind his veneer he has serious emotional problems.

My last job in the crime solving business occurred four weeks before my departure, exactly on January 16 and for which I received accolades which were like a coronation before my going away.

In the phase of my new existence as a retiree (Oh boy do I hate that word!), Caroline, my wife, and I are in a period of adjustment, not knowing exactly how my retirement is going to play in our relationship.

We always got along very well, paradoxically, because we didn't see each other often. I worked about 10 to 12 hours a day, sometimes including holidays; my leisure time during weekends was erratic, controlled by the demands of my work. Caroline is the sole owner of Peninsula Gift Shop, a unique store that sells all kinds of original objects manufactured by the people of Seattle, including notepads, ornaments, calendars, copies of the first Eye Chart created by Dr. Franciscus Donders, to name just a few of their two hundred and fifty products. Caroline attends her shop five and half time days a week.

We cherish our time together. Our bond is strong, our love unconditional.

I don't know how the new circumstances may affect us; life is unpredictable.

One day, we were planning to have lunch at the Three Sisters Bakery, but before she asked me to drive her to Alki to pick up a box of new jewelry, which she was planning to sell in the store.

I parked my car on the street and waited patiently for her to finish her task.

Seldom have I had time to reflect upon my life. Now I have plenty of time to mull over my future.

I was wondering how frequently would I be driving my wife to her errands, or shopping or going to the movies. None of those chores are appealing to me. Perhaps we will go to China. Here is where my fictional hero, Bao Gong An, uncovered the most mysterious cases; the only thing I didn't like about him is that he executed the criminals he caught using a guillotine.

As my mind was wandering I was contemplating the beauty of the neighborhood; the houses with water views from the adjacent river; the new restaurants and the new Library, which was in the final phase of construction.

I noticed that the car in front of mine had an expired license tag, but that was none of my business. I was a detective and not a traffic enforcer. Some cars did not respect the bike lane; again, that was not my concern. A couple with their two lively twins were walking down the street in a very animated way, the postal carrier was delivering mail, and an old couple who wanted to cross the street before the walk sign went on were stopped by a responsible citizen and that produced a humorous quarrel.

Caroline took much longer than I expected, which reinforced my purpose of not becoming her driver.

A few minutes later, the situation changed. I picked up my cellular phone, dialed 911 and told the dispatcher to send a patrol car for a Code 6AD. A Unit arrived within one minute. I identified myself, but since I worked in another District, they did not know who I was. Upon my insistence, they called my old precinct and that prompted respect followed by immediate action.

We started to chase the mail carrier, who was carrying his mail bag. Two of us, civilians, on foot and two patrol cars made sure that the suspect would not fly. We got him within five minutes; mercifully when the gentleman was asked to drop the bag and lift his arms, he did not resist.

The other detective, Jason Lipps, read him his Miranda rights and proceeded to inspect the bag, which contained valuable jewelry, silver candelabra and a stack of money.

Before saying good bye, the Alki detective invited Caroline and me for a cup of coffee. He remembered who I was and told me that he was honored to be in my company.

He was curious how I reached the conclusion that the man was committing a crime. *What were the clues that I had to assert that a misdeed had been perpetrated?* he asked.

I explained that as I was waiting in the car I noticed among other things the presence of the postal carrier; when I saw him for the second time I realized that the bag he was carrying appeared much heavier than before, contrary to what one may expect if he had delivered his load.

It was then when I called 911.

After his praise we exchanged visiting cards and departed the amiable gathering, promising to see each other again.

Then I said,"Ah, by the way Jason, today is January 16, Martin Luther King Day, and Postal Offices are closed."

The imaginary patient

Good morning, everybody. As you know, our company, Stewart and Associates, Inc., is dedicated to serve only Pharmaceutical Companies in the US and abroad. Our task as a PR firm is to enhance their financial returns to a maximum, the same commitment as other similar organizations.

Today, we are going to discuss how we are going to differentiate ourselves from them and the strategies that will make us the premier Healthcare Communication agency in the world.

Our first obligation should be directed toward ourselves; that is the reason that I decided to reorganize our firm. We will downsize from 80 to 30 people; doing so will enable us to function in a very effective way; this will give us the opportunity to excel, and become again the recipient of the TFD Industry Award.

Before I get to the core of my talk I would like to inform you that starting today you will become partners at different levels with an immediate increase in salary ranging from 10 to 35 percent.

We have renewed contracts with the four more profitable Pharmaceutical Companies of the world. This is a challenge and a great responsibility; in order to accomplish our mission I decided to implement a new program. The achievements could be unprecedented and will place us as the number one PR Company in the United States.

The information I am about to provide you is FYEO; a minimal transgression of this tenet will be enough grounds for dismissal of the transgressor.

The Pharmaceutical Industry bestows an indispensable, valuable service to the people; not only are they the providers of life-saving medications, they also through R&D introduce new drugs to treat new and old infirmities.

Before I introduce my plan, which entails making sure that our four clients maintain a leadership position through their increasing revenue and political decisions, take note of important data which will help you in the understanding of the direction that our Company will be taking.

Statistics are boring and tedious and yet necessary. Detailed information is included in the Handbook that will be made available to you at the end of my presentation.

The following is a brief summary of its content:

There are 233 great categories of diseases. The subclasses in each one bring the amount of medical conditions to several thousand. The prevalence and incidence is enormous; they are outlined in the Handbook.

To illustrate just a few: there are 75 million persons in the United States afflicted with hypertension; 32 million with Chronic Obstructive Pulmonary Disease; 26 million people with Diabetes; 230,000 will be affected with prostate cancer in the next 12 months and 216,000 will develop breast cancer. There are 1,000,000 people with AIDS. Three million persons suffer with Rheumatoid Arthritis, 1 percent of us are bipolar and 15 percent will become depressed at one time or another. Every year 1,000,000 patients will develop gallstones and 150,000 Colon Cancer.

In essence: **there are more medical conditions than people, since many are troubled with many ailments at the same time**.

This suffices to point out that Pharmaceutical Companies, if well managed, have the potential of becoming the most profitable corporations in earth.

And yet that is not so. Pfizer only made 10 billion dollars, while Exxon Mobil made 41 billion in 2011.

Until recently Pharmaceutical Companies have directed their efforts to increase the selling of medications to treat conventional diseases, only to find that competition is very strong and the market is 'limited'.

In addition, many conditions are disappearing or becoming less frequent thanks to new medical advances, vaccines and technology. It follows that in order to preserve financial gains the Pharmaceutical Corporations must find new ways to expand profits.

Drug manufacturers have been able to increase the volume of sales by increasing the consumption of medications. This is achieved by Direct-To-Consumer Advertising or DTCA in media outlets, especially television (a $3 billion a year market), identification of target audiences and digital marketing through the Internet. Social networking disguised as Consumer Protection Agencies are also a way to reach vast audiences.

For our clients to boost their earnings, which last year reached 170 billion dollars out of the 500 billion in sales from all pharmaceutical industries, we need to find new ways to increase their sales. How?

The answer is simple and uncomplicated. Innovation is the name of the game.

There is a plan in action to **medicalize physiological conditions**. One of the most successful new invented diseases is the Premenstrual Dysphoric Disorder (PMDD). This 'condition' is a change in the nomenclature of premenstrual tension, a complex, multifaceted syndrome, which used to be a stage in the ovulatory phase and now has been converted into a **Medical Condition**. Before enthroning premenstrual tension into a disease, women managed their condition with diet, rest and exercise and only those with severe symptoms received treatment. Today, premenstrual tension has become a *true* medical condition - again, we call it PMDD - and not a phase of the menstrual cycle, and is affecting millions and millions of women. Drug manufacturers have been able to lodge this concept in doctors' brains, through Physician Relation programs and other means and as a consequence they feel compelled to treat it with medications in millions of women, which translates to millions of dollars in sales for drug manufacturers. This new entity has been recognized as a medical disorder - thanks to our lobbyists - by the Food and Drug Administration (FDA), the influential government agency.

In contrast, the Committee for Proprietary Medicinal Products (CPMP) - let me say it from the start, our enemy - stated that PMDD is not a well established disease, warning women with mild to moderate pre-menstrual symptoms to avoid Prozac (the treatment of choice), which they deem inappropriate and risky. Prozac has serious side effects, like an increase in the risk of suicidal ideation in young females or sexual dysfunction in others, for which reason they asserted that this medication should be reserved only for very severe cases. CPMP claim that aggressive promotion and marketing makes otherwise healthy women consume medication, with its inherent risks, that they don't need.

This dispute should, with other help, be won by the Pharmaceutical Companies, since it is easier for doctors to prescribe a drug than spend time counseling a patient.

There is a big crusade in Europe against the use of Prozac, claiming that PMDD is not a proven established medical identity. We, being marketing experts, have the obligation to denounce the statements of CPMP and the Europeans as hogwash since they go against the interests of drug manufacturers. Physicians and patients should be made cognizant that PMDD is now listed as a depressive disorder in the *Diagnostic and Statistical Manual of Mental Disorders,* and this will give more weight to our position.

Zoloft and Paxil have been added to the list of medications to treat PMDD.

In essence: a new disease has been created, a boost to medication consumption, ergo increase revenue.

A fierce detractor of the use of new drugs to treat 'new' medical conditions wrote:

"Medicalization of habitual life situations is one of the more dangerous artificial creeds created by drug makers. Grief caused by the loss of a loved

one has been transformed into a depressive condition requiring antidepressant medication; occasional disinterest in sex, because an individual may have other things in his mind, like difficulties in his job, financial problems, bad relationships or whatever, has been labeled as sexual impotence requiring Viagra; sexual difficulties by women led to a new syndrome, a situation that can be cured with a testosterone patch (more about this later), which is now a one billion dollar market.

All these inventions ignore the complexity of life circumstances, where not only biological but psychological, situational, cultural, environmental and existential factors play a role.

Aging manifestations like osteoporosis, diminished stamina, wrinkles, fat belly, blood pressure, cholesterol level, and sleeping difficulties are considered medical entities, treated with medications, ignoring better alternatives like, for example in the case of osteoporosis, exercising and a diet rich in Vitamin D and calcium and sun exposure. Insomnia managed by sleeping pills instead of stress reduction is an example of the overuse of drugs. There is a new class of medications like Ambien, Lunesta and others which should be used only for very short periods of time, such as when traveling or preoccupied by recent concerns: unfortunately, there are many using these drugs on a regular basis, not taking into consideration the harmful side effects like behavioral changes, abnormal thinking and sleep driving, to name only a few of the reported collateral problems.

Bayer is targeting the weariness that most of us experience when we wake up in the morning by aggressively advertising Bayer AM, an over the counter pill that contains aspirin and caffeine. Aspirin can cause gastrointestinal bleeding among other side effects and caffeine can cause cardiac arrhythmias. To be more emphatic: medications can help, medications can kill. Inventing new diseases brings a huge, profitable market to pharmaceutical companies; the disregard of concerns about safety and benefits is appalling. It creates a civilization of legal drug takers, which is as bad as the one of illegal drug consumers. In most instances what is needed is lifestyle modification."

Those detractors are our adversaries, imperil free enterprise and are true obstructionists. They claim that they are protecting the health of others, when in reality the Pharmaceutical Companies are the ones promoting wellness.

To validate their claims, they point to the fact that the drug industry has paid billions of dollars in fines and indemnification because of their misuse or the deaths that the drugs have produced. Although true, errors and death represent the price that many times we pay for progress. The Pharmaceutical manufacturers have a motto: 'Make one billion, pay one million, case closed.'

It is our obligation to allow the treatment of medical conditions without impediments, no matter what the consequences.

Physicians should consider Menopause, not as a stage in life, but a medical disorder; depression, even if circumstantial or temporary, should be considered a disease amenable to medical treatment.

High Cholesterol, Hypertension, Anxiety, Attention Deficit Disorder should remain solid medical sicknesses. Pre-Hypertension should be treated with medication instead of lifestyle modification; people with normal cholesterol should be counseled to take statins to prevent plaque formation which leads to obstructive coronary disease, even if in many cases the collateral damage produced by them may be fatal; Attention Deficit Disorder should be extended to adults and not confined to children like in the past. Anxiety should be replaced by a term with a better medical connotation like Social Anxiety Disorder. Attaching the word Disorder or Medical Condition, gives otherwise superfluous symptoms a sense of chaos, disarray and mayhem that would require the use of drugs.

Moliere in his book *Le Malade Imaginaire* (the *Imaginary Invalid*) concocted a patient, Argan, a hypochondriac who had an addiction to doctors and a myriad of medications. He should be our hero, the icon of the Drug Industry. He and others like him are the ones that bring riches and prestige to the Drug manufacturers, companies that work tirelessly to promote the wellbeing of Humanity.

To finish and as an example of innovation and creativity, I will describe one of the latest achievements of drug manufacturers: The Low Testosterone Syndrome (LTS).

Testosterone is a hormone made by the testes in men and by the ovaries in women (and in small proportion by the adrenals) and regulated by the hypothalamus and the pituitary gland.

In males is responsible for the development of testis and prostate, phallic enlargement, deepening of the voice, fertility, muscle and bone mass and the growth of body hair. It delays osteoporosis and is essential for wellbeing; its effects are essential for the development of secondary sex characteristics.

These effects are undisputable. When used in younger men with hypogonadism, testosterone replacement is curative; unfortunately, there are not many patients that fall into this category, cutting into our profits.

But there is a very large group of people that we are now able to target who will become prominent users. They **will** suffer with **Low Testosterone Syndrome (LTS).**

To achieve this goal we will need to convince doctors and people alike, through vigorous advertising campaigns, that there is such an entity.

Who are the potential people afflicted with LTS? Everybody (or at least everybody until testosterone becomes generic and non-profitable).

Let me explain: As part of the aging process people complain of lack of stamina, decreased sexual libido, diminished muscle mass, preclinical depression, decrease in facial and body hair and osteoporosis. Coincidentally, these are the same symptoms that are present in younger males (a small group) with severe forms of hypogonadism, where there is a definitive decrease production of the hormone; in this last, small group, all the changes can be substantially reversed by testosterone replacement.

We know that the concentration of testosterone declines 1 to 2 % per year after it peaked at age 20 to 30. A normal, physiological process! This means that a man of 60 has a concentration of testosterone that is at least 60 to 70% below that of a 25 year old.

But if we communicate, with no hesitation, that low testosterone, although a sign of the normal aging process, is reversible, we will convince people that they may achieve the fountain of youth by taking testosterone in the form of injections, gels or ski patches.

Let the scientists decide: 1. What is the threshold to define low testosterone? 2. Does the syndrome really exist? 3. What is the contamination by contact affecting others? 4. Does biologically active testosterone correlate with concentrations of total testosterone? 5. Are there any studies comparing one group of old people receiving testosterone with one receiving placebo? 6. What are the long term side effects?

The side effects are between 1 and 6%, and they include problems with urination, acne, breast enlargement, allergy, worsening of sleep, headaches, nausea, vomiting and mild fluid retention and most of all it may fuel the growth of prostate cancer, induce the formation of clots in the legs that if dislodge may cause pulmonary embolism and death, and heart attacks, among others.

Testosterone applied on the skin may be transferred to children, who may experience enlargement of the penis, increased libido and aggressive sexual behavior; while women may experience growth of body hair and acne.

Until those questions are answered we are placing Testosterone on the front burner and selling billions of dollars a year.

The task of a Marketing Company is to create favorable financial conditions for their clients, leaving to scientists the discussion of science.

I foresee new Medical Disorders such as: laughing or crying too much; sleeping more than 8 hours a day or less than 6; anxiety while watching a movie; blushing; shyness; temerity; cowardice; inability to concentrate; not achieving goals in life; not able to excel in tennis or golf; talking too much on a cell phone; texting in excess; needing too much love or being reticent to being loved; having a short fuse or being too patient; having too many or few friends...

We will call this new type of drugs **Lifestyle Modification Medications.**

In the meantime, let's go to work. You have the best tools at your disposal: create new brands, use the media and the Web, create public forums, produce new marketing plans, brainwash the malleable brain of physicians and most of all, construct communication programs.

The Kingdom of others

The Horse and the Bee

"How lucky you are,"

The bee said to the horse.

Why is that?

"Because you live thirty years

Or more."

And you?

"A few weeks at the most

Unless I am a queen,

Which I am not."

But you are lucky in other ways,

Are you not?

You feed on nectar of flowers;

I eat only grass.

"You are fast.

I have two pair of wings

But have a short flight."

You make honey,

Sweet and sunny;

You are a pollinator

And open the buds of flowers.

"But the crab spiders

Hide in the blossom

To catch me.

It is awesome."

You are so industrious,

So social, so diligent.

"So are you my friend -

A symbol of valor,

Strong and handsome:

You walk,

You trot,

You race,

You gallop,

When threatened,

You fight or flight

You are smart."

You are so kind,

But now,

If you don't mind,

It is time for my heraldry."

The Lion and the Eagle

You are majestic,

You big cat.

Do you have any friends?

Yes, many.

I am a lion.

Live with my lionesses.

Together, we hunt

Prey,

Eat.

We sleep in the prairies

And

With the tigers,

I made ligers;

With the leopards,

Leopons;

With the jaguar,

Jaglons.

I envy your strength,

Your poise.

You are the king of the jungle,

The emperor of beasts.

But you, big eagle,

Are a bird of prey:

Strong,

Powerful,

With keen eyesight,

Free to fly,

Catch your quarry,

Heavy or light.

You mate for life;

You share the nest

To protect your heirs,

Feed your young

Until they are

Big enough.

You are splendid,

Strong and wise.

You are a predator

And so am I.

The Dolphin and the Tortoise

I like to learn

To play like you.

They say you evolved

From a mammal

Of the land.

Is that why you are so smart?

You are fast

When you swim;

Your hearing

Lets you know

Shape and form.

Well,

You cannot smell.

You cannot have it all.

You can live one hundred and fifty years,

Protected by your carapace.

I am so amazed

What do you do

Inside your shell?

Do you feel well?

You eat so much grass

You eat so much weed -

To what end?

To be wise

To be sturdy and robust,

And yet

You are so slow

With no place to go.

They say you are

Gifted and bright,

Social and kind,

Helping your friends

To breathe.

Protecting humans from sharks

By swimming in circles around,

And yet

At times

Hostile and bad,

Hurting other dolphins

Or killing your child.

What a contradiction!

Most of the time

Playful and kind

Others

Mean and harsh.

The Rabbit and the Cat

You live in the meadows

Or in a burrow,

Your hideaway

From foxes and badgers.

How grand!

You have a baby

Once a month,

You eat grass -

Is that why

You ran so fast?

May I share with you

What you have?

Your long ears,

Your soft fur...

Oh don't feel good for me.

I can be food meat

Or become a scarf or a hat,

Not like you, happy cat

That everybody loves.

They spoil you;

They give you food,

Clean your waste.

You can see in the dark,

Hear many sounds

Smell all smells.

Be my friend;

Touch my nose.

Have no fear,

My affection is here.

The Man and the Woman

What have we learned?

Are we hawks?

Are we doves?

Strong as lions,

Smart as dolphins,

Warriors like eagles,

Fast as a horse,

Slow like a turtle,

Preying like cats,

Laborious like bees -

Are we good?

Are we mean?

Why do we kill?

We smile,

Laugh,

Cry;

We rape,

Steal -

We are bad;

We help;

We give;

We love;

We heal;

We are good;

We are fine;

We are kind;

We create,

Write,

Paint,

Build,

Think,

Act.

We care;

We don't care.

We provide;

And take away.

We are evil;

Make war.

More and more,

We can be better

Than that.

The uncontrollable persistence of a routine

Contrary to what the title of this article appears to suggest, this is not a psychological or philosophical essay but rather the vicissitudes of Greta, a 50 year old lady. Her story shows that fate is determined by our temperament, not by luck or divine intervention.

Greta was born in a remote country where the air was pure, the waters clean, the environment unpolluted, the streets were paved, and sidewalks swept every day, driveways were free of debris and trees trimmed. Homes were well kept; hers was particularly tidy and neat. Living in such a place morphed her character. For Greta, wars existed only in the pages of the newspapers; famine, poverty and disasters were abstract concepts.

She married well, lived in a nice neighborhood, had two children delivered almost painlessly and devoted her life to her family.

Her house was spotless, no dust. Beds were fixed as soon as everybody was up; the kitchen utensils were always sparkling. The clothes in the closets were sorted out by color and season. She scrubbed the dishes by hand, no matter how many were there to clean.

She extended her ways everywhere she went. When Paul, her husband, and Greta were invited for dinner to a friend's home, she would try to help the host to wash the dishes after the meal was over, usually to no avail.

When something was out of order at home, she would whisper some untellable words and proceed immediately to restore things to their place.

Her family and friends tried to convince her to loosen up, with no success. Paul and the kids, after many years, decided to let it be; after all, her ways made her happy.

One unlucky day, Greta was hit by a car while crossing a street, although she had the right of way. She was admitted to Intensive Care at St. Mary's Hospital. She improved slowly; her doctors were confident that she would recover and would have no neurological deficits. The medical plan was to reduce the sedatives little by little and remove her off the respirator.

I don't know if it was Destiny or the Twisted Finality of Obsessiveness: that morning she woke up and started looking at the surroundings; she noted the monitors that were showing her blood pressure and pulse rate, a screen showing the oxygen saturation of her blood, and three IV bottles hanging from a pole. There was a machine that she had never seen before, with two hoses attached. She noticed that one of them appeared to be curled, while the other one was in a straight position. Instinctually she wanted to place one near the other, so both would look nice and proper in a clear 90 degree angle with the machine. In spite of her weakness she put so much zeal in her effort that one of the hoses became dislodged, interrupting the flow of air to her lungs.

They placed her in the coffin wearing an immaculate white dress without wrinkles; her hairdo was neat and tidy. She had a big smile on her face, a smile that said: mission accomplished.

Three Centuries

Next month you are going to be 114 years old, a super centenarian. You have lived through three different centuries. What are your thoughts about being one of the very few that have reached this age in a world of seven billion people?

That is a nonsense question. It's like asking me how do I feel that I am breathing or that my heart is beating or my kidneys are filtering blood. Being 114 years old is who I am. You can change your question by asking if, as one of the few, I still feel strong, alert or the like.

What is the secret for reaching the one hundred mark with your mind intact?

I don't have any recipes for my long life or the long life of others; honestly, I don't think that it matters because whatever it is it cannot be replicated. You better ask the researchers who about three years ago came to my home and asked me to give a blood sample to measure all kind of things, from vitamin levels, enzymes, immunological traits, to genetic studies. A few months later they came back and told me that they could not find the secret of my longevity and asked to be allowed to take biopsies of my skin and aspirate my bone marrow. I refused - what is the point? Why would people want to live longer than they should?

Have you been able to cope with stress better than others?

I know where you want to get, but let me tell you that you will not find one single aspect in my life, not my social status, my eating habits, my sex life, my sleeping patterns or my heritage - that may explain my longevity. It is better to accept that it is just serendipity; I am at the other end of the Bell curve, as simple as that.

How many descendants do you have and are you able to remember their names and faces?

I had six children and three of them are alive. They had twenty-four children of their own. This twenty-four had a total of 70 children. I remember the names of my children and their children but the names of the others many times escape me. My youngest son Bill came up with the idea that each time any of them would come for a visit, they would use a shirt or a polo with their name printed on the fabric. That precludes any misgivings. About a year ago one of my great-granddaughters got married at the Luxor Gardens and as an homage to me the entire family decided that they would respect the tradition; during the wedding the boys wore black pants and a white polo with a logo bearing their first and last name and the girls the same. Those who were not related dressed casually; they may have felt bad for not being part of the family. It was a memorable wedding, one that I will never forget.

Do you fear death?

This question arises all the time, mainly from people like you; it is inconsequential. It seems more that death fears me than the other way around since it has avoided me for all these years. I find fascinating that there are many books written about aging and death, some by prestigious writers. I have glanced through them; they are cathartic but do not add much to the paradigm of living. I appreciate Joan Didion's loss of her husband and daughter and her writings; she combines words that result in incredible prose and poetry; the content, though, never leaves a mark on me. I have already been there. Others talked about death casually, like Julian Barnes, when he was making arrangements for his mother's funeral. Others use the fear of death as the element that separates believers from non-believers.

People should use whatever makes them feel good about their mortality; talk, read or write about it; no matter what, it will come announced or unannounced - it is not our choice.

Are you an atheist, an agnostic or a God-fearing creature?

Is there any other category left? I have a new one for you: I do not care about it.

And why should I? If there is a God, He does not need me to reaffirm his existence, and if there is no God my beliefs do not matter.

You have lived through several wars, big ones and little ones - how did they affect your sensibilities?

There are no big or little wars. They are all substantial. They are a reflection of the hidden devil within us. They are a sign that we have not yet left the notion of tribalism in whatever scale. War is perpetual; you won't be able to name a period of time when there were no wars. As with death we write about them, despise them, and yet they seem unavoidable. Some time ago we learned that a war that will end all wars does not exist; the best we can do is to terminate them the best we can and be ready to avoid or eradicate the next one.

Our readers would appreciate some words of wisdom from you; after all, you are unique. Being 114 years old puts you in a position that none of us have.

People have contributed to mankind in different ways; somehow you probably have something to say to future generations to

placate the evil inside and let the angels take over.

What I am about to say has been said by many before me. Being immortal is a curse and not a blessing. If not, ask The Wandering Jew or Raimon Fosca, the protagonist of Simone de Beauvoir's novel *Tous les homes son mortels*. To be mortal is a blessing. What matters is how you live your life and not how long you are going to live. Recognize your existence as it relates to you and others. Living is a responsibility, a duty to which you are accountable. If you allow others to live in poverty, not to have access to medical care, to forfeit an education, a roof under their heads, recreation or go hungry, you will be untrustworthy and you will die a thousand times. Commitment to do good to others is an absolute value that cannot be tampered with. Life is an enterprise; you are free when you accept the freedom of others. Your freedom does not come casually, but rather with obligations toward you and your contemporaries. You have to commit to live a life where the word standstill has no place. You don't need to transcend. The Kingdom of Heaven is the Heaven within us. Dying means that we have lived before, living means that we are going to die. The clouds announce the rain to come, the rain reveals that the sun will rise again.

Death is us.

Welcome Back Salomon

My name is Greta Wenzel, the owner of Trio Art Gallery in Vaduz, which I opened in 2010 as a retort for not having been invited to join the Board of Directors at the Kunstmuseum in Lichtenstein. The Gallery is comprised of three sections: one houses my Private Art Collection, the second is dedicated to one single painting, which is usually borrowed from one of the leading art museums of the world, and the third is reserved for local new artists.

The admission charge is 12 euros, which I donate to Briggs Art School, an institution dedicated to the development of visual arts, painting and sculptures.

Recently Elizabeth, a 14 year old patron, told me that she did not enjoy her visit to our latest show; she politely asked me if I could reimburse half of the 12 euros she paid as compensation for her disappointment. I was taken by surprise, thought about her request and confess that I did not know if it was a fair petition. I didn't want Elizabeth to have as I did a doubt about the morality of her request, so I called Salomon.

Salomon, upon learning the quandary asked: *Elizabeth, if you had enjoyed the exhibit **beyond** your expectation would you have offered to pay Greta an additional 6 euros?* The girl responded, "*No.*" *Then*, said Salomon, *you are not entitled to a partial refund.*

Why I worship my psychoanalyst

I tried so hard. I wanted to emerge sane from my inner struggle, but shadows and darkness prevailed. I went back to that period of my life when I was about 10 years old when frequent nightmares populated my nights. My mother would die; my brothers disappeared in hollow, unending precipices. Caves were filled with monsters suffocating my senses and I wouldn't survive. I didn't know why I was having these delusions; there were no threats to my existence, my parents were caring, always guarding their three sons from unexpected tempests; their life was dominated by their concern toward us; they sheltered us from hunger, harm and despair. We called that love, which we reiterated again and again, with words and deeds.

Little by little something persuaded my ghosts to leave and the nightmares disappeared, until now.

There are no monsters or caves any longer in my nights, only despair for being in a locked place without doors, no entries no exits - only me, nobody else.

Why a return to the nocturnal miseries of my childhood? What happened then? What is happening now? I don't know. I am happy; perhaps I shouldn't be.

In the real world, I am where I am because of my sense of determination, or so I believe.

Perhaps I am hounded by doubts, which I don't perceive.

My father, the strong icon in our family, was known by everybody as a man of rectitude, high ethics and impeccable behavior. He was named the executor of the will of an old friend Isaac, 20 years his senior. Isaac was leaving all his possessions to her sister Gertrude, who at the end of her life became demented and was living in a nursing home. If she were not to survive him, the assets were to be dispersed to the Masters-Wong Foundation, one that was close to his friend's heart. A week after Isaac died his sister passed away. My father made the arrangements for the funeral and services for the departed and disbursed the assets of the deceased according to his will. Or it appeared to be so. It was a complicated task because Isaac had many possessions and he had to arrange the sale of the assets; after paying taxes the money left, which was substantial, was to be dispersed to the Foundation.

When Dad died five years later, he left a considerable fortune to his three sons. My brother Richard, who worked with my father, and was well acquainted with the family financial situation, summoned my younger sibling Jack and me, to tell us that it was very strange that we inherited such a vast amount of money. He went over the books very carefully and could not find the source of Dad's wealth. He believed that Isaac may have had some hidden funds and that our father took illegal possession of them. In addition, an original Renoir that Isaac owned, valued in the millions, could not be accounted for.

Richard was not absolutely certain that Dad committed such deception, but it was enough to plant a seed of misgiving in our mind. We became distraught with the idea that our idol could have committed such an act of wickedness. If we were to take possession of an ill-gotten inheritance, that would make us complicit.

We, the three brothers, decided to preserve our moral principles and gave away to charity what Richard considered was not ours. We still inherited a considerable amount of riches.

For a while I was demoralized; but as is always the case, life went on and apparently my angst disappeared. After a while nothing perturbed the tranquility of my days, but then slowly something started agitating my nights.

Were the memories of my father's supposed folly coming back? Or was something else haunting me?

I am not lying on this couch to defend my actions as a matter of logic or morality; I believe that my convictions are ethical, sometimes divorced of the opinion of others. I don't claim to possess the truth, to be smart or trying to be judgmental of others. I don't feel that my deeds need validation; they are part of the zigzags of life.

I don't need my acts to be sanctioned by you; I don't need you to tell me that they are right or wrong.

I have an urge to know, that deep inside, I approve of the actions I have taken in the past and to know if they are contributing to my horrific hours of darkness. If I wouldn't be having these recurrent nightmares I wouldn't be here.

I am surprised that some of my actions could be perceived by my inner self as an act of depravity.

As you know, I am a famous journalist. At the beginning of my career I reported many events around the world. I became well known when I was covering the first Persian Gulf War and then the siege of Sarajevo. Many people accused me of not being an objective journalist because I was not only reporting but also giving an opinion in the gruesome massacre of the Bosnian Muslims. I was, they said, to reserve any commentary on the conflict for myself.

Later, I did memorable interviews from Palestine, Israel, Afghanistan, Pakistan, Lebanon and Iraq. When I was wounded by crossfire I returned home, had to convalesce for nine months, and in deference to my family decided to end my assignments as a war correspondent and became a political analyst.

It is known by everybody that I hold strong progressive opinions and have clashed publicly with many figures of the right. I am not combative by nature but I have no patience with the stupidity of others.

Last September, two months before the election in Texas for US Senator, one of my sources informed me that George Fioli, the Republican candidate had a torrid love affair 12 years earlier with a lady named Gloria. After so many years she was willing to come forward with the story; she may have had her reasons, but that was of no concern to me. I was assured that the account was true and easily verifiable. She had kept a lot of documentation that proved without a doubt her version of the events.

Fioli was somebody with an ideology that I despised. He was a member of the NRA, with an extreme opinion about gun control. He wouldn't compromise an iota in passing any legislation that could prevent mass shootings. If he was in the pocket of gun manufacturers, I did not know. He was adamantly opposed to any kind of sensible immigration reform. He had been married for fifteen years and had no children; I found it surprising that he was opposed to birth control measures of any type. During his first term he had approved legislation that was overly protective of banks and corporations, with clear detriment to the working poor.

His opponent Marcus Murray was a Democrat, a veterinarian and a war veteran who devoted all his life to helping others through civic actions. I knew him well and shared many of his convictions.

Fioli and Murray were neck to neck in the polls. It was clear that exposing Fioli's past follies would most likely sink his chances to become elected.

This election was very important because it was going to change the majority in the Senate, perhaps with terrible consequences.

I was tempted to denounce his previous folly with Gloria and then let the election run its course. I explored other aspects of his life. Although his policies were abhorrent, he was a lawful man; his political policies did not infringe any criminal or civil laws. His past relationship with Gloria was a personal matter that had nothing to do with his political ideology. One may say that having an affair denotes a serious flaw of character; I was not convinced. Flaws are part of human nature. I was not ready to judge him or others in matters of the heart. Who knows what was going in his life at the time he was with Gloria? I was not about to get immersed in this issue.

I wanted Fioli to lose the election but could not bring myself to make him fail by accusing him; namely when I did not subscribe to norms of the society based on social convention or religious principles. I never had been judgmental of people's behavior in their personal spheres. His affair was a personal matter, it occurred 12 years ago and to bring it back to life after such a long time would be a perverse calculation.

The electorate would have to decide to vote for him based only on his political beliefs and proposals.

Was it justified to use whatever it took to make him fail in his aspirations? I felt that if I were to denounce him that would make me a vigilante, which I despised. Nobody should impose ethical principles on others.

It had been done before; journalists had uncovered a multitude of scandals that have ruined the lives of many and in the meantime made them famous or rich.

I decided not to expose Fioli, who went to gain the election by a narrow margin.

Time passed, and his record in the Senate showed that his positions were among the most reactionary that have ever been documented in the US Congress.

Is now the time to expose his past so he would be forced to resign his position?

I cannot bring myself to decapitate him; we should fight ideology with deeds and words.

Perhaps these two dilemmas, the one related to my father and the one about Fioli, keep my phantoms locking the door at night. I am thoughtful that it is not easy for me to accept dad's misdeeds, if there was ever one; it is not that simple to allow Fioli to exert the power he has to hurt others.

Who gave you and your brothers the power to determine that your father had indeed committed a perfidy of such magnitude? You have portrayed him as somebody with impeccable conduct; after his death, you decided that he might have embezzled money that was not his.

Do you realize the moral arrogance that it takes to decide that he was guilty of a questionable crime? Once you and your siblings decided to give away part of his fortune, the uncertainty of that deed became a fact. You and your brothers have judged and by doing so brought ignominy and disgrace to the ethical fabric of a man that was dead and could not reply to an accusation of that magnitude.

You may believe that by giving away the supposed booty your honor and integrity would have remained intact, and yet it is the exactly the opposite. It shows that you care more about yourself than you care for others. You place yourself as the owner of firm, unbreakable principles, you perceive yourself as whole and complete in the sphere of moral principles, eager to protect them even if it destroys the reputation of others. Why do you need to reinvent yourself as a pure and honorable man? Could it be that deep inside you feel that even the part of the 'clean' inheritance that corresponded to you was money that you did not earn, thus it did not belong to you and by finding a justification to dispose of part you are entitled to keep the rest?

It looks like you have to construct a world without human frailties. Does it not occur to you, a person who has seen the ravages of war, the cruelty of others, the horrors of senseless battles, that goodness does not come just in one size, that the human condition has thousands of shades that are ever changing? From this kaleidoscope we pick what suits us and should not condemn others for having different choices.

What is it that forces you incessantly to discern what is good or bad, what is right or wrong? In your quest you look like a butterfly, flying without direction.

Is it okay for people to have a little bit of malice or envy? Can we lie, use pot, imitate others or cheat without you exiling us to a kingdom where only ignominies exist? Can you give us a license to live an imperfect life?

You have displaced your father from a site that may have belonged to him.

Why have you and your brothers removed him from his pantheon?

You need to have a better comprehension of who you are and look at the world like an outsider. A blind person can discover the shape of things by touch but cannot appreciate color. When it comes to ethics we are like the blind, able to understand the world in few dimensions only. There is no moral absolutism.

What bothers me more is the second part of your narrative, the one you brought to light because somehow you feel it may be responsible for your stormy nights.

You have created another quandary in your life, guided by the imposition to live the life of the virtuous. You aspire to have a blameless conduct, to be respected and live a life without reproach, at all cost. During your career you have risked your life in the battlefront, as a journalist your duty has been to inform, even if by doing so you were going to encounter death or injury. You are a brave man. You do what you think you have to do.

But you feel that your primary obligation is first toward yourself and here is where you are wrong.

You are right that what Fioli did 12 years ago in his life is irrelevant to his current political behavior; this is without discussion. Perhaps Fioli showed a lack of integrity or a weakness of spirit when he had an affair. Perhaps we could assume that his infidelity and betrayal denotes a lack of a solid moral fabric. Perhaps not. We don't know the circumstances of his actions. And furthermore, who are we to decide that having a lover, an act that goes against the established principles of our society, is an immoral act? Who says that one cannot love two persons at the same time? Who has established the dictum that we have to repress our natural inclinations, instincts and desires?

But this is a subject for another discussion; at this time not important in the realm of analyzing your deeds.

You are aware that Fioli is an individual who by legislative actions may inflict pain to large segments of the population. It is not an exaggeration to claim that by defending the interests of the corporations he will cause harm or even precipitate the demise of many. He brings havoc, ruins lives, and halts the progress of young people who aspire to get an education. He curtails the access of many persons to health care by being on the side of the medical insurance companies whose main objective is financial gain, independent of the fate of individuals. We both know of hundreds of stories of patients being denied services who end up dying. You and I know that he doesn't give a damn about the environment and sees all proposed legislation to improve our living conditions as a threat to the fiscal wellbeing of the energy companies. Fioli believes in a society of castes and has no trepidation to do what he has to do to defend the one that he belongs to. The rich class, in his understanding, should be the rulers of society. They should be protected and honored as in times past. He and his acolytes, of course, don't talk on those terms because they are aware that a society of castes is an anachronism, but they have found a way to disguise their intentions by claiming that everybody should aspire to have as much as they have. If I tell my servant: keep tendering to me and don't worry about your present conditions, just remember that one day you could be like me, this will appease him and he will keep performing his subservient functions.

Study after study has shown that most of the people born in a poor family will remain poor, uneducated, have an increased incidence of incarceration, use more drugs and commit more crimes. A testament to this is that in the United States there are more than two million people in jails and more than 1.2 million are Black or Hispanic; a disproportion to the amount of whites. To make things worse, the middle class, previously with better mobility, is now shrinking because of the unfair distribution of wealth.

As a political analyst you know of all these facts and this should have been enough to bring his affair to the public attention to prevent Fioli from being elected.

But you chose to do otherwise. Your moral judgment was more important than the common good. You did not want to betray your principles, even if it meant placing the lives of others in jeopardy. The defense of your moral principles was above any other consideration. It was you first, and then everybody else.

As with your father, what really mattered to you was to live by your inflexible codes. You, who appear to be so adventurous, accept social dogmas without allowing yourself to doubt if they are always right or if they could be broken for something more important. Nobody is asking you to break the law, but you should be eclectic enough and help diminish the ills of our society.

John Morley tells of Diderot's protestation in the case of:

> *... a certain cobbler of Messina that saw his country overrun by lawlessness. Each day was marked by a crime. Notorious assassins braved the public exasperation. Parents saw their daughters violated; the industrious saw the fruit of their toil ravished from them by the monopolist or the fraudulent tax-gatherer. The judges were bribed, the innocents were afflicted, the guilty escaped unharmed. The cobbler, meditating on these enormities, devised a plan of vengeance. He established a secret court of justice in his shop; he heard the evidence, gave a verdict, pronounced sentence, and went out into the streets with his gun under his cloak to execute it. Justice done, he regained his stall, rejoicing as though he had slain a rabid dog. When some fifty criminals had thus met their doom, the viceroy offered*

a reward of two thousand crowns for information of the slayer, and swore on the altar that he should have full pardon if he gave himself up. The cobbler presented himself and spoke thus: "I have done what was your duty. 'Tis I who condemned and put to death the miscreants that you ought to have punished. Behold the proofs of their crimes. There you will see the judicial process which I observed. I was tempted to begin with yourself; but I respected in your person the august master whom you represent. My life is in your hands; dispose of it as you think right." Well, cried the abbé, the cobbler, in spite of all his fine zeal of justice, was simply a murderer. Diderot protested. His father decided that the abbé was right and that the cobber was an assassin.

This happened in the context of France's moral corruption at that time. So who was right, the cobbler or the abbé? Was the cobbler a revolutionary, an agent of change, a crusader, an advocate for the common man, a protector of defenseless women, and a zealous defender of the property of others whom we should exalt or condemn?

I am asking from you to put your social ideals beyond your rigid ethical tenets. Sometimes we have to give away your precepts to serve your cause and the cause of others. I am not saying that you should subvert the established social order but I am suggesting that you do what Picasso did. He was a realistic painter trough his earlier days but then he started experimenting with different techniques and developed the art form of Cubism. It was combinations of creativity and imagination

292

but mainly of daring that allowed him to revolutionize plastic arts.

The locked room from which you cannot escape has a key that will open all doors; don't look beyond yourself, because it is within you. Just remove the carcass of your moral constraints and you will find it. It is not easy because our principles are the reason why we are who we are. When they change, we change. At the beginning of the process we will feel desolate, bare, unprotected. We have removed the pillars of our foundation and will have to start anew.

Made in the USA
Lexington, KY
28 October 2013